HERE WE GO

SHANNON STACEY

HERE WE GO

A hockey player climbing back to the top of his game blows up the sport's hottest rivalry when he unknowingly indulges in a one-night stand with his rival's sister.

Kristen Burke isn't a hockey fan. She grew up in the shadow of an older brother destined for the Hockey Hall of Fame and she wants nothing to do with hockey players. She's focused on her career and nailing the promotion she's worked hard for. She also likes to have a little fun, but when the hot, bookish guy she brings home for a night turns out to be her brother's fiercest on-ice rival, all that work might be for nothing.

Will "Cross" Lecroix is stuck in a city that hates him, doing a conditioning stint after an injury incurred during a fight, and a quick fling with a beautiful woman seems harmless enough. Not even twenty-four hours later, he's in the media spotlight sporting a bruised jaw and being asked if the rumor he spent the night with Erik Burke's sister is true.

Making a split-second decision meant to save her reputation with her conservative boss, Will announces he and Kristen have been dating. With her promotion potentially at risk, she has no choice but to play along—and the playing part isn't bad at all. The more time they spend together, the more the line between pretend and real blurs, but Will's return to his team looms over them. As the clock runs out on their fake romance, they have to decide—is what they have the real thing, and is it worth the price they'll pay?

A SECOND SHOT

Included short story sequel!

Andi Morgan was the one who got away—the woman Erik Burke walked away from to focus on the game—but when their paths cross once again, all he wants for Christmas is the chance to take another shot at love.

(Previously published in the Hockey Holidays anthology.)

HERE WE GO

*B*reaking news: the Baltimore Harriers announced today *that Cross Lecroix is out indefinitely due to the shoulder injury he sustained after dropping gloves with Erik Burke in last night's heated overtime loss. #NoCrossNoCup #MaybeNextYearHarriers #HottestRivalryInHockey*

⁓

THREE MONTHS LATER...

"YOU LOOK like you spent your entire day trying not to wring somebody's neck."

Kristen Burke slid onto her usual seat at the bar—on the end that wrapped around, so she could see everybody in the Firewall Bar & Grill—and picked up the vodka soda her favorite bartender set in front of her. "Nobody knows me like you do, Zach."

"What is it you do again? You work in an office, right?"

She sipped her drink, pondering her answer. She was

the unofficial office manager, as well as handling social media and promotion, for a very conservative boss with some political clout because it had been the best job opening for her overpriced degree and the most in line with her future goals, but she'd been working on her exit plan for a while. Once she was *finally* promoted to *official* office manager and he made that run for mayor he was gearing up for, she was going to be his chief of staff. And then she intended to use the experience and the contacts she gained to get a similar position with somebody whose personal views didn't make her want to sit at this bar and have a vodka soda every night after work.

"I *manage* an office," she said, but she really didn't want to talk about it. "It's boring and my boss is an asshat. What's good tonight?"

"There's a beef stew special in honor of it being freaking freezing outside, but based on the reactions I'm seeing, I highly recommend the salad."

She laughed. "A salad sounds good. With some grilled chicken on top."

"Sure thing."

Left alone to sip her drink and let the annoyances of the day slip away, she looked around the bar. It wasn't very busy tonight since the more casual patrons were probably staying home, out of the bitter cold, so if he was here, she wouldn't have any trouble spotting him.

And there he was, sitting at the same table he'd been at two nights ago. Thick brown hair. A well-trimmed beard. Broad shoulders. She could tell he was tall, even though he was sitting down. And she knew from the one time he'd glanced up and they'd made eye contact on her way to the restroom that his eyes were very dark. So intensely dark she'd actually shivered.

"Do you know who that guy is?" she asked Zach once she'd finished the salad and he'd brought her a fresh vodka soda. "The one in the gray Henley shirt toward the back?"

Zach took a look and then shook his head. "Nope. I've seen him in here three or four times, but he's not chatty, and he seems to keep to himself."

Kristen wasn't surprised. Something about him, whether it was the way the soft cotton shirt hugged his body or the way he carried himself, suggested the man didn't quite fit in with this crowd.

Not that there weren't other attractive, leanly muscular guys to be found in the greater Boston area. But this particular watering hole attracted a techie crowd, and this guy was not only rough around the edges, but his phone appeared to be a generation or two out of date.

She'd seen him a couple of times before tonight, and she'd been interested since that first glance. He usually had a meal with a couple of ice waters, paid his bill, and then took his time nursing a coffee while looking at his phone. She was pretty sure he was reading, based on the rhythm of his thumb swiping, and she had a serious thing for guys who liked to read.

A few women and a couple of guys had tried to strike up conversations with him, and Kristen had been close enough to overhear a couple of them. He was polite and friendly, while making it obvious he wasn't looking for company.

A smoking hot guy who enjoyed good food, liked to read, and wasn't looking for an easy hookup was totally Kristen's type when it came to easy hookups.

"He pay with a credit card?" she asked Zach and smiled when he nodded.

He wouldn't give her any of the guy's information—and she wouldn't ask—but she knew Zach would take note of it, so if Kristen's judgment was off and something happened to her, the police would at least be able to identify the guy she'd last been seen with. It wasn't much, but it made her feel slightly safer, and it beat being in a long-term, monogamous relationship with her vibrator.

After paying her tab, she took her drink with her and made her way to the guy's table, coming to a stop in his peripheral vision. "What are you reading?"

He looked up, and she saw the flash of annoyance in his dark eyes before his eyebrow arched and a slow smile curved his lips. "A biography of Abigail Adams."

She snorted. "Sure you are."

He slanted the screen in her direction, so she could see the text. "Ask me anything."

"Where was she born?"

"Not far from here, actually. In Weymouth." He pushed the chair across the table from him out with a shove of his foot. "Have a seat."

A little bossy, but she didn't mind that in a man.

No, that wasn't true. She very much minded it, as a rule, but not from a man who was looking at her as if he was imagining what her naked body would feel like under him.

"I'm Will." He extended his hand across the table.

"Kristen." He didn't offer a last name, and she didn't ask. She didn't care. And she also didn't offer hers.

But she did take his hand, putting hers in his much larger one. It was less of a handshake and more of an excuse for physical contact, and the touch lingered as his thumb stroked over her knuckles. Even though he didn't squeeze, she could feel the strength in him.

"Okay, Will," she said, once he'd let go of her with visible reluctance. That was a very good sign. "What's a guy like you doing reading a book like that in a place like this?"

"I'm reading a book like this because Abigail was an interesting lady and my mom recommended it to me. I'm in a place like this because I heard a rumor they make grilled chicken that isn't over-seasoned rubber, and I keep coming back because the rumor was true and because I like hearing you laugh."

"Sweet sentiment, but I've seen plenty of women hit on you, and you always leave alone."

"They weren't you." He knocked back the last of his coffee and then leaned back in his chair. "You're always alone. No significant other?"

"No time for others, significant or otherwise. But sometimes I like company." At this point, if he didn't take the hint, she was walking away. "I'm really choosy about it."

"I've been told I'm pretty good company."

Judging by the confidence evident in his body language and expression, she was willing to bet he was more than pretty good and he knew it.

That was okay. She liked confidence in a man. Sure, there was a fine line between confident and cocky, but Will seemed to have his feet planted on the right side of the line. Barely.

"You have any plans for tonight?" she asked, ready to move the party back to her place. She wanted to touch him again and more extensively, and she wanted that touching to happen behind closed doors.

"I was planning to spend the evening with Abigail here," he said in a low voice, before he gave her a look that curled her toes. "But you are *far* more fascinating to me."

"I live a couple blocks away. If you can stand the cold, you're welcome to come keep me company."

"I'm pretty comfortable with the cold. Let me pay for your drink and we can get out of here."

"Thanks, but I pay for my own drinks. And I already settled up, so I'm ready when you are." She drained her glass and stood as he grabbed his coat off the back of the chair and slipped it on.

Zach gave her a thumbs-up on the sly when she walked past the bar to get her coat, and she was impressed when Will took the parka from her so he could hold it. Holding the cuffs of her soft, cream sweater, she shoved her arms into the coat's sleeves.

Then he gathered her hair in his hands, and she sucked in a breath as his fingertips brushed her neck in the process. Awareness of his body, so close behind hers that she could feel his breath as he tugged her hair free of her collar, sizzled through her. The anticipation of what was to come was delicious, and her hands trembled slightly as she zipped her parka.

The chivalry lasted throughout the short walk to her building. He held the bar door for her. He walked on the curb side of the sidewalk. And whenever the biting wind gusted, he'd try to adjust his pace to shield her from the worst of it.

So, Will was a gentleman in the streets, she mused as she let them into her building and nodded to the night security guard before crossing the lobby to the elevator. Hopefully he'd be just as attentive in the sheets.

"This is a really nice place," he said as he followed her down the wide, well-decorated hallway to her door.

"I like it." She figured he was probably fishing for more information about her. Like how she earned the paychecks that footed the bill for this apartment. Or whether she'd kept it in a divorce. She'd heard a few theories over the years, but so far none of her male visitors had guessed the truth. And she'd like to keep it that way. "Good security. Lots of cameras in the lobby and the hallways. Good amenities, too."

Will made a noise that sounded like agreement, but he didn't push the subject. He either didn't care how she'd come to live here or he'd already figured out if she wanted to say more, she would.

Kristen liked that about him. She liked a *lot* about him, actually. As she glanced at him while unlocking her door, he watched her with those dark eyes and gave her a wicked grin that practically took her breath away.

She was definitely looking forward to getting to know him better.

WILL LECROIX WASN'T sure what to make of the tall and very shiny building his new friend brought him home to, with its security desk and pass-carded elevator. She'd seemed more like the artsy loft type to him, and he'd been hoping he wouldn't have to deal with a roommate situation. He was too old for that shit, and being shushed during sex was a serious mood killer.

Not that he was particularly loud, but he really hoped he was going to hear Kristen yelling his name into her pillow tonight.

He followed her into her apartment, standing to one side so she could close and lock the door, and looked around. The mystery of Kristen deepened. The place was immaculate, with high-end fixtures and one hell of a view of the city behind the large window. It looked like a large, open-concept, studio-type apartment, with a couple of doors on the back wall he assumed led to the bedroom and bathroom.

But rather than being filled with the kind of expensive

décor that always made him afraid to make himself at home lest he knock something over, Kristen's home was sparsely decorated with battered leather furniture that looked good quality and comfortable but definitely had some years on them.

"You can hang your coat up if you want," she said, pointing into the closet where she'd just hung hers.

"Thanks." Now came the awkward transition time between the pickup and the bedroom, he mused as he put his phone, keys, and wallet in his coat pockets and hung the garment on an empty hanger.

"Would you like a drink?" she asked, and there was nothing awkward about the way she looked at him. She wasn't nervous or trying to figure out the next step. She just wasn't in a hurry to get on with it. "I have vodka, coffee, and water."

He chuckled. "I'll take a glass of water. I'm a decaf-after-dark kind of guy."

"Noted." She walked toward the refrigerator. "Make yourself comfortable."

Choosing the corner of the sofa that allowed him to watch her fill two glasses with ice and water from the fridge dispensers, he did as he was told.

He'd eaten at the bar his first night in the city, on the recommendation of some of his teammates who knew Boston well. Finding a place with good food where he would go totally unnoticed could be hard at times, even when he wasn't in Baltimore, so he'd been happy with it at first. Then he'd seen Kristen walk through the door and became an instant regular.

There had been eye contact the second night, when she'd been on her way to the ladies' room, and he'd seen the interest. But he hadn't approached her or struck up a conversation because the last thing he needed right now was any kind of a relationship. It might vent some of his pent-up frustrations, but it wouldn't be fair to a woman who was looking for more.

When she walked over to his table tonight, any willpower he might have been able to summon was depleted the second he looked up. Her soft sweater and well-worn jeans hugged ample curves his hands wanted to explore, and the athlete in him had been just as aroused by the challenge in her bright blue gaze.

Can you handle this?

He was sure as hell going to try.

Kristen handed him one of the glasses before sitting in the other corner of the couch, slightly sideways so she could see him.

"I don't really care what you do for work or what your zodiac sign is," she said, and he appreciated the bluntness. They were both on the same page, then. "But what I do want to know is if you usually choose where you spend your evenings based on rumors about their grilled chicken."

"Good grilled chicken is hard to find." It was one of the truest things he'd ever said. "Good grilled chicken I can eat while watching you? That I'll keep coming back for."

"If I hadn't joined you tonight, how long would it have taken you to approach me?"

He probably wouldn't have, no matter how badly he wanted to talk to her. If she wanted his company, she'd let him know. He'd been expecting a flirtatious smile or a tip of her head toward the empty stool next to her, but instead she'd made her interest a little more plain. He liked that about her.

"I would have worked my way around to it," he said, not wanting her to feel as if he would have just passed her by.

And maybe he would have broken his own rule and approached her eventually because she was *not* a woman a person could keep passing by. "I didn't want to be pushy."

"I don't mind pushy." She paused to take a sip of her drink, still watching him over the rim of her glass. "Just be prepared for me to push back."

Anticipation flooded his veins as she stood and took the few steps needed to close the distance between them. She set her drink down and then took the water out of his hand. When she set the glass next to hers, he assumed she'd take his hand and lead him to her bedroom, but she hooked her thumbs in the waistband of the soft, black leggings she was wearing and peeled them down before kicking them away.

Catching a glimpse of silky black panties when she threw one leg over his, Will ran his hands over her thighs as she straddled his lap. His fingertips pressed into her soft flesh, denting her skin, and his dick strained against his fly.

She pulled the sweater off and flung it away, treating him to the sight of her pale skin covered by a cream-colored, lace-trimmed bra before she leaned down and covered his lips with hers.

He closed his eyes, her mouth claiming his as his hands roamed her soft, curvy body. She was lush and perfect and the way she moaned when his thumbs brushed over her taut, fabric-covered nipples seemed to vibrate through his entire body.

This, he thought, was going to be so worth closing his book for.

2

The man certainly knew how to kiss a woman.

Kristen let herself savor the sensation of having a man under her. It wasn't a pleasure she indulged in often, so she intended to enjoy the hell out of this one while she had him. His kiss was demanding, almost rough, and his fingertips bit into her thighs before his hands slid up to cup her breasts.

She expected him to go right for the clasp, but he ran his thumbs over the satin fabric, making circles around her taut nipples. Then he pinched, almost painfully, and she moaned against his lips.

In case he was waiting for permission, she unclasped the bra herself before undoing the lower two buttons of the Henley shirt. She wanted him naked sooner rather than later.

He didn't pull the straps down and fling the bra away. Instead, as she broke off the kiss and straightened her back, he slid his hands under the fabric and cupped her breasts again before slowly drawing the straps down her arms. She watched him stare at her body, and his expression left no doubt he was very into soft curves.

When his mouth closed over her nipple, she ran her fingers through his thick dark hair before stroking the side of his beard. It was soft, not prickly, and she was looking forward to feeling it on the inside of her thigh.

He sucked hard, and she gasped, her hips rocking against his. The sound he made low in his throat thrilled her, and she decided it was time he lost some clothes. Like, all of them.

As his mouth moved to her other breast, she gathered the hem of his shirt and pulled it upward. He pulled his arms out of each sleeve as she held it, and then he caught her nipple in his teeth for a second before lifting his head.

She flung the shirt away and gave herself a few seconds to enjoy the look and feel of his muscular chest before climbing off of his lap. He took her hand and pushed himself off the couch, and she led him toward the bedroom.

"I don't usually pack condoms to read my book, so I hope you have some," he told her as they crossed the threshold to her room.

"I do," she said. More than enough to get them through several rounds if he had it in him. And she really hoped he did. "So it's safe to lose the pants."

There was enough light shining in from the living room so she could appreciate his sculpted ass and thighs as he stripped the rest of his clothes off. He even had amazing calves, which she noticed when he removed his socks.

Then his hands were on her again, and he kissed her as he backed her toward the bed. She explored his body with her hands—his chest and his back before sliding her hands down to cup his ass—while his tongue danced over hers and his hands caressed her breasts.

Once it was within reach, she broke off the kiss to open her nightstand drawer. She withdrew a condom packet and tossed it on the table before closing the drawer. It was kind of a test—would he pick it up right away or let it wait while he got to know her body better?

And the man passed the test.

Ignoring the condom, he lifted her onto the bed and, after stripping her of her panties, got to know her very thoroughly. His mouth and his hands moved over her, and he took his time with her breasts. The hollow of her throat. Her shoulders. He kissed his way down her stomach as his hand slipped between her thighs and stroked her. Then he hooked one hand behind her knee and opened her to his mouth. She'd been right about how good his beard would feel against her thighs.

He not only knew where to find the clit, but he sucked and licked with just the right amount of pressure, and the orgasm hit her hard and fast. Her fingernails dug into his shoulders, and he soothed her with gentle strokes of his tongue before he kissed his way back up her body.

"It's been a while," he said, giving her a sheepish grin. "So tell me now if there's another condom in that drawer or if this is my only shot."

"There's more," she said, and she snagged the wrapper off the nightstand to hand to him. "I want you now."

It only took him a few seconds to roll on the condom, and then he covered her body with his. She ran her hands over his chest, liking the way he held eye contact with her as he guided the tip of his erection into her.

He took his time, easing into her slowly then backing off before pushing a little deeper in slow, even strokes. Kristen wasn't sure if he was making sure she could handle it or if he was trying to exercise some self-control, but she liked it.

His muscles were hard under her touch, and she loved skimming her palms over the chiseled curve of his ass.

When he was fully inside of her, Will paused, lowering his head to suck first one nipple and then the other before nipping at the side of her jaw. She turned her head, capturing his lip between her teeth before kissing him.

Finally he started moving with long, steady strokes that gave her the delicious friction she'd been craving. He looked down at her, the corners of his mouth turned up as he quickened the pace, and she moaned.

Each stroke came harder and faster, until she could feel the tension growing inside her again. Reaching between their bodies, she scraped her fingernails over his hip bone and skimmed them over his balls before pressing her fingertips to her clit.

He thrust hard into her as she came, and she dug her fingers into his biceps, her back arching off the bed. As the waves of pleasure subsided, she felt him shudder, and he groaned as he came seconds later. He pushed into her, holding there while his hips twitched and his breath came in ragged gasps.

After a few seconds, he reached down to hold the condom and pulled out of her before rolling and flopping onto his back. Kristen listened to their breathing as it slowly returned to normal, and she liked the fact he slid his hand toward her until his pinkie was hooked over hers.

"There's a box of tissues on the nightstand and a trash can under it," she said in a still slightly breathless voice.

He rolled away for a moment, and then he stretched out on his back and tugged her close. She rested her head on his shoulder, running her hand over his chest. It wouldn't be comfortable for very long, but it wasn't as if she was going to fall asleep like this.

She didn't want him to fall asleep, either—not only because she wasn't finished with him yet, but also because he wouldn't be spending the night. Usually this was where she'd get up and throw her robe on, and then ask him if he'd like a drink before he called for an Uber. But she didn't want Will getting out of her bed yet, so she figured conversation might keep him awake until round two commenced.

"I'd never seen you at Firewall before and then you're there three nights in a week. What made you suddenly pop up like that?"

"I'm in Boston for business."

"Oh? And what is it you do?"

He chuckled. "I thought you didn't care about my job. Or my zodiac sign."

She trailed her fingernail down his sternum. "I find you a little more interesting now than I did when I said it."

"Okay. I'm a Scorpio. And I play hockey."

"Shit." She sat up, pulling the sheet over her breasts. "*Shit.*"

He snorted, obviously amused. "Scorpios aren't as bad as they say, you know."

This couldn't be happening right now. She'd finally met a man she already knew she wouldn't tire of after a few dates and he was a freaking hockey player.

"Hockey?" she asked, just to be sure. Maybe she'd heard him wrong. "Really?"

"Yes, really. You asked what I do, and what I do is play professional hockey. Minor leagues at the moment, but not for long."

"I should've known when I had my hands on that ass you played hockey. Dammit."

He sat up, though he didn't get out of her bed. "Most

women *want* to fuck professional hockey players, you know."

"I'm not most women. I hate hockey, and I don't fuck hockey players."

"Didn't."

"What?"

"You *didn't* fuck hockey players. Past tense. Now you do."

"*Did*." She gave him a pointed look. "Past tense."

"Ouch."

"My brother plays hockey."

"Really? Like in a local league?"

She slid off the bed, letting the sheet fall away so she could pull her robe on and signal he should get dressed. A hockey player? Not a chance. She was done here, and it was time for him to go. "No, professionally. For the Boston Marauders."

She happened to be looking at him when she said the words, so she saw the effect they had on him. His face froze, the color draining from it, and she was willing to bet if she could see the back of his neck, the hair there would be standing up. "Your brother plays for the Boston Marauders?"

"Yeah. Erik Burke."

He stared at her for a few long seconds and then fell back onto the pillow. "Oh, *fuck*."

OF ALL THE women in all the gin joints in Boston...or something like that.

Will scrubbed his hands over his face as he tried to figure out how the hell to get out of the predicament he'd gotten himself into. He'd just had sex with the sister of the only guy he'd ever really hated off the ice—the guy with whom he had a rivalry so infamous nobody talked about one's career without at least a passing mention of the other.

He needed to get the fuck out of here and forget he'd ever met this woman.

But he didn't want to. He didn't want to leave yet and even though the sweat had barely dried on his skin, he already knew he wasn't ever going to forget her.

"What's going on right now?" she asked, and he sighed, surrendering to the inevitable.

"Does the name Cross Lecroix mean anything to you?"

She rolled her eyes and made a sound that told him yes, the name meant something to her. And it wasn't something good. "Of course. It wouldn't be a Burke family dinner without a heaping side of Cross Lecroix hate."

It took everything he had not to laugh out loud. Not that there was anything particularly funny about the situation, but the improbability of them ending up in bed together was so ridiculous he could barely hold it back.

Before he could speak, she pointed a finger at him. "If you're about to ask for an autograph or help getting to the majors or some bullshit, you can get up and get the fuck out right now. You're not getting to either of them through me. Not my brother and certainly not Cross fucking Lecroix."

That did make him laugh. *Cross fucking Lecroix?* But he stopped laughing when she sent an icy glare his way.

"I don't want an autograph." He got up and pulled on his boxer briefs because it was time to get dressed. The way this night was going, he was going to be out the door pretty damn soon, and he'd prefer to be fully dressed when it slammed behind him. "Do you not even know what Lecroix looks like? You haven't seen a picture of him? Seen his face on the television?"

"Not that I remember or paid any attention to. I might

have to listen to my family bitch about him, but other than that, I ignore him. I ignore *all* of it." She frowned, and then he could practically hear the click of puzzle pieces falling into place in her mind. "No. Absolutely just...no."

"I swear I didn't know who you are." He really hoped he could make her believe this was nothing but an accident, even though he could barely believe it himself.

"You said your name is Will."

"It is. Will Lecroix." He shrugged. "When I was a kid, I had a bad habit of cross-checking, and with the name Lecroix, it became a nickname. By college, nobody was even using my real name anymore. Except my mother and sister, of course."

"You said you play in the minor league."

"And I also said not for long, and I meant that literally. I'm in Boston for a conditioning stint with the Skimmers."

She cinched the belt on her robe tight and then exhaled slowly. "This is bad."

He couldn't disagree with that, but only to a point. "Getting naked with Erik Burke's sister is definitely right up there on the list of sins I shouldn't have committed, but I'm having a hard time being as sorry about it as I should be. Tonight wasn't *all* bad."

When she put her hand over her mouth and then turned her back, Will decided to give her a moment. It was a lot to digest. But when her shoulders started shaking, he mentally ran through every curse word he knew and shoved a hand through his hair.

Goddammit, he'd made her cry.

Because nothing about their interaction tonight—as focused on the physical as it might have been—led him to believe she was a woman who cried easily, dark thoughts crept into his head, and his fists clenched at his sides.

Maybe Erik Burke was even more of an asshole than he'd thought. Or their old man. That guy was a real piece of work, from what he'd seen and heard over the years.

The thought of her being afraid of the men in her own family turned his stomach, and he'd closed half the distance between them before he realized she wasn't crying.

She was laughing.

And he didn't know what to do with that, either. How the hell had he gotten himself into this predicament? And maybe the better question was how he was going to get out of it. Or did he even want to?

He didn't find it quite as laugh-out-loud funny as Kristen seemed to, but of all the people in the world he could have had semi-anonymous sex with, Burke's sister had to be the least likely. And if he hadn't already met her, the very suggestion of such a thing happening would have sent him running like his ass was on fire.

But he had met her. He'd met her and wanted her and, if he was honest with himself, he already wanted her again.

"It's tempting to think you set this up somehow," she said when the laughter had passed. "But I saw your face when I said Erik's name, and there's no way you knew."

"What would I get out of tracking you down and then sitting there by myself, reading a book and minding my own business until you decided to have sex with me?"

She snorted. "Just to piss off my brother? Remember, everything I know about you has been filtered through my dad and Erik. Does your mom sit around talking about what a sweet boy Erik Burke is?"

"I wouldn't say she's a big fan, no. Especially lately."

"Yeah, about that." She tilted her head. "Didn't you get hurt? I mostly tune out the hockey talk, but I have a vague memory of my dad and Erik talking about him taking you out of the game."

Ouch. "They were probably just excited because with me out, the Marauders might have a chance to win something."

She arched one eyebrow. "Seriously? I have zero interest in this macho bullshit, in case that wasn't clear before. I'm merely curious because I heard you were injured, but you didn't seem to be hurting tonight."

"It was just a separated shoulder that had nothing to do with him." He threw the words out casually, but he shuddered at the memory of how the nagging pain had become a *searing* pain when he was swinging at Burke and turned into a flaming agony when they went down on the ice and Will took both their weights on his shoulder. It had *everything* to do with Burke. "I'll be doing a conditioning stint with our affiliate team here in Boston after the All-Star break, and then, if I'm still pain-free, going back to Baltimore."

"Huh." She chuckled. "I feel like there's some irony in your team's minor league affiliate being here in the city that hates you."

"Yeah, I know. But it's not like the teams had a big rivalry umpteen years ago, when that decision was made. That's centered more around me and Burke...uh, your brother."

"I need a drink," she announced.

"I wouldn't turn one down myself, unless you're throwing me out."

"I'm not throwing you out." He would have grinned, but she cast him a hard look over her shoulder. "*Yet.*"

3

Cross Lecroix was in her apartment. Not only was he in her apartment, but not too long ago, he'd been in her bed.

Wrapped in her bathrobe, Kristen curled up in the corner of her sofa, once again facing Will, who'd sat in the other corner. They each had a fresh vodka soda, with an emphasis on the vodka, because what the hell had even happened tonight?

There was no way she could have known the hot guy in the gray Henley reading a biography of Abigail Adams in a Boston bar was the man her father and brother hated more than anybody else. Hating Cross Lecroix was like the family legacy—any night the Marauders lost sucked, but if Lecroix's Harriers also lost their game, it wasn't all bad.

Trying to wrap her mind around Will and the notorious Cross being the same man had her sipping her drink again, watching him over the rim of her glass.

"You're not going to run your mouth, are you?" she asked after a few minutes of sitting in silence that was more contemplative than awkward.

"What do you mean?"

"I mean, you're not going to use this as some kind of trash-talking weapon in your hockey war with my brother, are you?"

He looked so shocked and offended, she almost felt bad for voicing her concerns. "Okay, I get that we don't actually know each other all that well, so I'm not going to get mad about that, but no. I wouldn't do that to you. Or to him, to be honest. Family's a line you shouldn't cross."

"Okay. It's just that I have a very conservative boss, and I'm up for a promotion I've worked my ass off to get. The last thing I need is to be caught in some one-night-stand sex scandal with the most hated athlete in the city."

"Maybe not the *most* hated athlete." He scowled. "Probably top five, though."

"You're top three on a good day. And you getting caught defiling Erik Burke's little sister would totally knock the other two out of contention."

"Defiling?" He laughed, shaking his head. "I'm pretty sure *you* defiled *me*."

"Possibly." She shrugged, and her robe slipped down her shoulder a little. She was going to fix it, but Will's dark eyes locked on the skin it revealed, and she left it alone. "It was something of a mutual defiling, but I doubt Boston hockey fans will see it that way."

"So, what now?"

That was a good question. If she had any sense, she'd not only tell him to call an Uber but make him wait in the lobby for it. Then she should forget she'd ever met the man, because nothing good could come from letting this situation go on.

But he was already here. She'd already had sex with the

official family nemesis, so what harm could a little *more* sex do?

"I think, when you're done with your drink, we should go back in the bedroom and finish what we started."

He downed the last of the drink in three swallows and set the glass on the coaster. "I'm done."

Since she was naked under the robe and he was only wearing boxer briefs, they didn't waste any time hitting the sheets. But the rush stopped there, apparently, because Will once again took his time lavishing his attention on pretty much every part of her body. At first, impatience distracted her—she really wanted his dick inside of her right now—but his mouth and hands were hard to resist and finally she let herself relax and revel in the feeling of being worshipped.

But when he finally reached for the condom, she waited until he had it in his hand, and then she shoved at his shoulder and laughed as he rolled onto his back.

"You in a hurry?"

"You have other plans?" he responded as she straddled him.

"As a matter of fact, I do." And she set about seeing how patient *he* could be.

She kissed his throat and his chest, swirling her tongue around his nipple before continuing down his body. His breath caught audibly when she reached the soft skin of his lower abdomen, and she grinned at him before sliding her palm up the length of his erection. His dick twitched against her hand, and she curled her fingers around it so she could close her mouth over the tip.

He groaned, maybe cursed, as she sucked in his length. She gripped him with one hand while she splayed the other over his stomach, holding him still. His body trembled when she stopped to run her tongue from base to tip before taking him in her mouth again.

It wasn't long before he growled and, taking her under the armpits, hauled her up the bed. She laughed and rolled away from him, but he caught her and jerked her onto her knees, giving her a sharp slap on the ass.

"Hey! Just in case you get carried away, my safe word is *icing*." She turned her head so she could see him and laughed at the look he gave her. "Hey, it makes sense. Like you overshot my comfort zone."

"I don't get carried away. Also, that's a pretty strange safe word for a woman who hates hockey."

"It's individualized, just for you. And it amuses me to think you'll never play hockey again without remembering how it feels to fuck me."

His hand fisted in her hair, and he pulled her face close to his, arching her back so his mouth was near her ear. "I'll be lucky if I can ever close my eyes again without remembering how it feels to fuck you."

Then she felt his hand brush against her clit before he drove into her from behind. She cried out and couldn't stop the moan of pleasure when he pulled almost all the way out and then thrust again. His hand was still tangled in her hair and he pulled it, making her push hard against him.

Her fingers dug into the sheet, and she would have buried her face in the pillow to muffle her cries, but he had her hair, exerting a constant pressure that increased almost to the point of pain when she dropped her head.

Over and over he drove into her, deeper and faster, until she wasn't sure she could take it anymore. And then he reached around and stroked her clit, and she might have screamed—she didn't even care—when the pleasure blew her world apart.

Her body was still shaking when Will let go of her hair and turned her onto her side, one leg caught between his and the other draped over his arm, pulled up toward her chest. Three hard thrusts and then he came with a guttural groan and pushed hard into her, his breath blowing in hard puffs across her heated skin.

As his body started to go limp, he withdrew and sank to his side so she could untangle her legs from his. She heard a couple of tissues being pulled from the box, and then his body wrapped around hers. He kissed her hair and her neck and her shoulder—a dozen tiny kisses.

"Holy shit," she whispered.

"Same," he whispered back, still trying to catch his breath. Then he kissed her shoulder again. "You are one hell of a beautiful woman, Kristen Burke."

Even though she was pretty solid on the whole loving-her-curvy-body front, the words still made her smile because they weren't just words. He looked at her like she was beautiful, and she could feel it in the way he touched her.

She was glad she hadn't sent him home when she found out who he was, because Will "Cross" Lecroix fucked even better than he played hockey, and the man was bound for the Hall of Fame.

As her breathing slowed and muscles she knew were going to be the delicious kind of sore tomorrow relaxed, she snuggled deeper against him and closed her eyes. It was the opposite of what she should be doing, she thought. She should be getting up. Offering him a goodbye drink. But she liked the feel of his big, hard body spooning hers.

She was going to get up and send him on his way...in just another minute.

~

WILL WAS ALMOST asleep when he heard a sound that had him wide awake again. "Was that your front door?"

Kristen lifted her head off his chest as a man's voice called her name from the living room.

"Oh shit." She scrambled off the bed and pulled on her robe. "It's Erik."

Oh shit indeed. "How did he get in?"

"He's my brother. Security doesn't pay any attention to him, and he has a key."

"And he doesn't knock?" They were both out of bed now, speaking barely above whispers.

"He's supposed to, but sometimes he forgets. He always texts me to tell me he's coming over, but my phone is...shit, in my coat pocket probably." She tied the knot in her robe's sash with a quick yank. "Stay here."

"Kristen, are you here?" Just hearing Burke's voice grated on his nerves.

"Hold on," she called before turning back to Will to hiss, "Do *not* leave this room."

They'd get out of this, Will thought as he pulled on his boxer briefs. Burke never had to know he was here.

But as Kristen told her brother to maybe knock first because she had company and reached back to pull her bedroom door closed, the angles of her apartment betrayed them. Will snatched his shirt off the floor and stood just in time to get a glimpse of the living room in her bedroom mirror, where he looked Erik Burke's reflection right in the eye.

"What the fuck?" he heard as the door swept closed, breaking the unfortunate eye contact.

"Erik, don't!"

Will heard Kristen, but there was no way she was going to keep Burke from coming through that door, so he tossed his shirt onto the bed. He wasn't going to face the guy with his arms stuck half through the sleeves.

Sure enough, over Kristen's loud objections, Erik Burke opened the door and walked in. His face was red, his mouth was twisted in fury, and his hands were already balled into fists.

Well, shit. This was going to hurt. "Look, man, I didn't know Kristen was your sister when I met her."

"You fucking liar. I kicked your ass and put you out of the game, so...what? You go after my sister for payback, like a little bitch?"

"Erik, he didn't know. Neither of us did."

"Stay out of this, Kris."

"Stay out of it? You're in my *bedroom*, dumbass."

"Let's take this in the other room," Will said, keeping his voice reasonable.

"How about you just get the fuck out of here?"

Will could hear Kristen's voice explaining to her brother that she decided when her guests should leave, but his gaze was locked with Burke's, and it wasn't in his nature to back down. "Seems to me I'm the only guy here she actually invited in."

The blow landed just above Will's jaw and even though he'd been braced for it, the pain still shook him. His fist was already in the air because it didn't matter if it was on the ice or not, if Burke wanted to drop gloves, he was all in. But Kristen's hand hit his chest, and he wasn't sure if she was in the way or not, so he had to drop his arm.

Her other hand was on Burke's chest and that's who she was looking at. "Get out."

"Kris, you can't—"

"Get. Out." She shoved at his chest, though she couldn't actually move him. "I mean it, Erik. Go home right now."

"I'll walk you out," Will said, because as far as he was concerned, they weren't done yet.

Kristen swung her gaze to him. "You're staying here. You don't even have pants on, for chrissake."

Neither man moved, and Burke glared at him over the top of Kristen's head. "This is between us, Kris."

"Yeah, I know. Burke versus Lecroix or whatever. I don't care. I want you to leave right now, and if you say a single word about this to Dad, you're not coming back. I mean it, Erik. I will not speak to you again for a very long time."

This time she used both hands to shove at her brother's chest, and he took a step back. Then he spun and walked into the living room, with Kristen on his heels. Will followed as far as the bedroom door because he knew seeing him leaning against the bedroom doorjamb in nothing but his boxer briefs would piss Burke off even more.

"He's using you, Kris. To get to me." Even as he walked toward the front door, Burke wouldn't give up.

"I know it's hard for you to believe and Dad would say otherwise, but not everything is about you," Kristen said. "Goodnight, Erik."

"Goodnight," Will couldn't stop himself from adding, which earned him cold blue glares from both Burkes.

"You can't hide behind my sister forever. I'll see you on the ice, bitch." Burke pulled open the door but had to look back for a parting shot. "If you make it back."

Kristen winced when the door slammed behind her brother, and then she shot Will an annoyed look. "Did you really have to antagonize him?"

"Yeah, I really did. Especially since you got in the way of him and me working it out our own way."

"And people wonder why I hate hockey." She pulled out the freezer drawer and rummaged around, probably looking for a bottle of vodka. He had a strict one-drink limit, and he'd already had one tonight, but he could use a shot right now. "Overall, that went better than I expected it to, though."

He snorted and caught the bag of frozen vegetables she tossed to him. After grimacing at the package—now he knew who the one person that liked frozen Brussels sprouts was—he pressed it to his jaw. Yeah, that hurt. "You really think so?"

"The police didn't have to show up, and neither of you left in an ambulance, so yeah. It went better than I expected."

"You going to kiss my face and make it better?" he asked, hoping to move the conversation along and put Burke out of their minds.

"Nope. You're going to ice that for a few minutes, until I stop feeling guilty about it and I'm sure Erik's gone, and then you're going to get dressed and go home. I've had enough of hockey players for the night."

He couldn't say he blamed her, but he was still disappointed he wouldn't be waking up in her bed in the morning. Rather than push the issue, though, he respected her decision to end their night, and once the Brussels sprouts started thawing, he got dressed and let her walk him to her door.

The robe was flirting with falling off her shoulder again, and he tugged it up with a sigh of regret. "Do I get a kiss goodnight?"

"I guess one kiss goodbye won't hurt." Then she looked pointedly at the bruise developing on his jaw and smiled. "Not too much, anyway."

He'd caught the transition from kiss *goodnight* to kiss *goodbye*, but he didn't comment on it. Instead, he cradled the side of her face and gave her a thorough kiss he hoped she would think about for many nights to come.

Then he opened the door and stepped into the hall. "I'll be in town for at least a couple more weeks. Maybe we'll cross paths again."

"Maybe. But I wouldn't count on it."

The last thing he saw before the door closed was that arched eyebrow and slightly naughty smile of hers, and he got hard all over again as he walked to the elevator.

Maybe he wouldn't see her again and maybe he would. But it had for damn sure been one hell of a night.

4

Will woke up with a dick that ached almost as much as the side of his face, thanks to a dream that was already fading from his consciousness, except for a lingering impression of Kristen's mouth on his neck.

At least his shoulder didn't hurt.

That wasn't still true when, what felt like a million hours later, he finally walked out of the Skimmers' rink. It wasn't a problematic pain, but it let him know the morning of practice with the team, interspersed with check-ins with the team doctor and physical therapists, had been a lot. The Skimmers were going on the road for a couple of games, and he wouldn't be joining them, since he wasn't scheduled to play until after the break, so he had the afternoon to himself.

He planned to spend it standing under a scalding shower until the hot water gave out.

When he hit the street, a man who'd been leaning against a red sedan straightened, and Will recognized him as a sports reporter from *Hometown Hoser*, a very popular hockey blog and YouTube channel, despite the name. Or maybe because of it. "Cross!"

"Hey, Joel. Doesn't Boston have ordinances about loitering?"

Joel laughed at his weak attempt at a joke then held up his phone to show his thumb hovering over the voice recorder button. "You got time for a couple of questions?"

Time? Yes. The desire? Not so much. But it was part of the job and he had nothing to hide, so it would be standard. The shoulder was fine. Everything was fine. He was looking forward to rejoining the Harriers when his conditioning stint was over. "Sure."

"Is there any truth to the rumor you got that bruise on your face from Erik Burke after he found you in bed with his sister last night?"

Will brain seized up like an old car engine, and all he could think was *oh shit* and *the recorder's running*. Anything he said could and would be used against him in the court of the hockey fandom's opinion.

"Where'd you hear that?"

"Let's just say it was a source very close to the Burke family. Is it true Erik Burke interrupted your one-night stand with his sister by punching you in the face?"

That asshole. Her own brother had run his mouth. He had to have because only three people knew, and only one of them was angry enough to make the situation sound so damn sordid.

"That's not accurate," he said tersely, which wasn't exactly a denial. He didn't want to lie because he didn't know if Joel had voice or video proof of Burke spilling his guts. But the actual details weren't 100 percent accurate—he hadn't found Will actually *in* Kristen's bed—so he tried to walk that line.

"Then what *did* happen? It's pretty obvious *somebody* punched you in the face last night," Joel pointed out. "What didn't my source get right?"

Standing there with a bruised jaw and faced with a story that was essentially the truth to explain it, Will thought fast.

His mom had drilled a lot of life lessons into his head growing up, and she'd taken it up a notch as he prepared to go off to college as a top athletic prospect. Never disrespect a woman. And never, ever throw a woman's reputation under the bus to make your life easier.

I have a very conservative boss, and I'm up for a promotion. The last thing I need is to be caught in some one-night-stand sex scandal with one of the most hated athletes in the city.

Will didn't give a shit what was said about him—and he couldn't do a damn thing about the circus surrounding him and Erik Burke—but he could do something to stop rumors of a one-night stand getting out there.

"Kristen and I have been dating for...a while."

That threw the guy, but he rebounded quickly. "How does Erik Burke feel about you dating his sister?"

Had this jerk not gotten a good enough look at his face? "I think it's safe to say he didn't take the news well. But at the end of the day, it's really none of his business."

The sportswriter arched an eyebrow and Will's stomach sank. He was digging himself one hell of a hole here. "You don't think his sister is his business?"

"Of course she is. I just meant that she's an adult and I doubt she runs her dating decisions past him." He needed to get out of here. His rental car was only about fifty feet away, but Joel was following him.

"How long have you been dating? When did you meet? Have you met her father yet? There's been a lot of animosity toward you from Lamont Burke over the years. What does he think about you dating his daughter?"

It was going from bad to worse. He hit the button to unlock his doors and tossed his hockey bag in the backseat before pulling open the front door. Then he looked at Joel over the roof. "Look, Kristen's a very private person, and yeah, Burke got pissed and took a shot at me, but it's behind us and there's no story here. I'm asking you to just drop it."

But as he drove away and glanced in his rearview mirror, Will saw Joel typing something on his phone screen while practically jogging back to his car. There *was* a story there, and the reporter had no intention of dropping it.

Shit. Kristen might not follow sports, but *Hometown Hoser* had enough of a following that somebody in her life was going to see it. Her brother and her dad definitely would. Or, worst case scenario, Joel would reach out to her directly for a comment. While she was working.

Just the thought of her being ambushed with this at work made his stomach hurt.

He shouldn't have answered the damn question at all, but he'd been caught totally off guard. Even though the guy was an asshole, Cross would bet good money Burke wouldn't have brought his sister's name into the story, but somebody in his circle of friends must have run his mouth. And the team's PR people had never given him a script for what to say if you were asked about a rival punching you in the face for having sex with a member of his family.

Like a deer caught in headlights, he'd frozen. Then he'd said the first Kristen-shielding thing he could think of.

He could only hope Kristen understood. And that he could get to her before she saw it on Facebook or some shit. Unfortunately, the one thing they hadn't done last night was exchange contact information.

KRISTEN GLANCED out of habit at her phone when it buzzed on the edge of her desk, even though she was letting calls go to voicemail today. She had enough on her paperwork plate without giving people opportunities to add to it. But when the Firewall Bar & Grill's number showed up on the screen, she reached for it.

She had the number saved in her contacts for the occasional night she just wanted to grab takeout on her way home, but Zach had never called her before.

"Hey, Kristen. Sorry to bother you when I know you're at work, but gray Henley shirt is here looking for your contact info, and he says it's urgent."

Will? "Did he say why?"

"No, but he's standing here, and he's thinking about trying to take the phone away from me. I adore you, but he's a big boy, so if it comes down to a telephone tug-of-war match, I wouldn't put money on me."

"I'll talk to him."

During the seconds it took for Zach to hand over the phone, Kristen took a deep breath to calm herself. It was ridiculous, but as soon as she heard *gray Henley shirt*, her pulse had quickened, and she could feel the hot blush across her chest.

"Kristen?"

The low, sexy timbre of his voice saying her name did absolutely nothing to soothe her nerves. "Yeah. What's going on?"

"I need to talk to you."

There was nothing light or flirtatious about his tone. "Okay."

"Can you meet me for lunch?"

Startled, she looked at the clock. "That's basically *now*."

"I know. If you can't, then let this guy give me your number so we can talk privately, at least. It's pretty urgent."

She couldn't imagine what could have happened between last night and this morning that would put that almost-panicked tone in his voice. He hadn't even had time to get an STI diagnosis he'd be forced to share with her. Shuddering, she mentally reviewed the work left to do, but curiosity trumped duty.

"I can do lunch, but it has to be very soon and close to my office." She named an intersection that was well-known and close enough to her building to give him an idea of where she was. "Give me your cell number and I'll text you an exact location in a few minutes."

He rattled it off and had her read it back to him. "Okay, I'm in my car now. Text me where to meet you."

The line went dead before she could say goodbye, and his sense of urgency made no sense to her. A conversation that was both an emergency and required privacy? Sighing, she mentally reviewed the lunch options in the area and then called to reserve a table at a spot her boss frequented often for sensitive conversations. She didn't feel the need to explain Stan wouldn't actually be joining her.

She texted Will the restaurant's location, and he responded that he was on his way and would see her soon.

After straightening her desk in a futile attempt to settle her nerves, she claimed a personal emergency she had to see to and slipped out of the office. It only took her a few minutes to walk to the restaurant—and she knew, since he was coming from Firewall, that he'd be another ten minutes at least—but she didn't mind having some time to settle into the small table in the semiprivate alcove next to the kitchen.

By sitting on the edge of the seat and leaning forward,

she could watch the door, and the second Will walked through it, she could feel her need for him like a low, constant hum of electricity through her body.

Hers wasn't the only head turned as he moved through the restaurant with purpose. Will was a big guy, and the intensity in his expression and his movements—along with the bruising along his jawline—made him look like a predator as he followed the hostess through the maze of tables to the few booths at the back that were surrounded by paneling and vegetation, which offered the closest one could get to privacy in a Boston restaurant at lunchtime.

When their eyes met, Will smiled, but it didn't reach his eyes, and his jaw was tight. He bent and gave her a quick and very polite kiss on the cheek before sliding into the bench across the table from her.

She would much rather he'd kissed her like he wanted to devour her and then sat on the same side of the table, sliding in next to her and working his hand between her thighs.

What was the point of a semiprivate booth if they didn't do anything you couldn't do in public?

"Thanks for meeting me," he said after accepting the menu from the hostess and asking for a glass of ice water.

"To say it sounded important would be an understatement."

"Yeah."

Their server appeared with his water, and Will downed a third of it while Kristen ordered a bowl of soup. She wasn't sure she'd have much of an appetite after Will told her whatever he had to say, based on the tension emanating from him in waves, but this was the only lunch break she'd have. And as close as they were to the kitchen, there would be no wait for the soup.

"I'll have the same thing," he told the server, but Kristen wasn't sure he'd even heard her order.

"So, what's going on?"

He took a deep breath. "Something happened today, and I want you to hear it from me first."

A frisson of fear made her spine tingle. "You didn't hurt Erik, did you?"

"No." The look on his face when she said her brother's name made it clear he'd like to, though. "I got a little ambushed by a sports reporter today and told him you and I have been dating for a while."

Her mind went blank, because of all the things he could have said to her, confessing to lying about them being a couple was the last thing she would have expected.

The server chose that moment to show up with her tray, of course, and Kristen stared silently at Will while she set their soup bowls down and asked if they needed anything else.

"We're good, thanks," Will said, before snapping his napkin open and draping it across his lap. Once the server walked away, he looked back at Kristen. "On second thought, maybe I should have discouraged you from ordering the large bowl of very hot liquid you might want to throw in my face."

"You told a sports reporter you and I are dating. And have been dating for a while."

"Yes."

She unfolded her napkin and smoothed it across her lap, turning this unexpected development over and over in her head, trying to make sense of it. The most obvious explanation was that this man wasn't well, was going to fixate on her, and she was going to end up at the police station, starting a paper trail.

The gut instinct she'd always believed in had possibly let her down this time.

"The reporter knew about you and me. He knew Burke did this." He waved a dismissive hand toward his jaw. "He had the story of Cross Lecroix having sex with Erik Burke's sister and being punched before he showed up all in my face."

That made no sense to her. "How did he know?"

"I don't know. Somebody in your building? Maybe Burke went out with his buddies all pissed off and ranting about it and somebody talked. But he knew about us. And when he asked me about it, I could only think about what you said about your boss and your promotion. I couldn't do anything about the story being out, but I could kill the one-night stand angle and make the story less..."

"Sordid. Salacious. Scandalous." She could come up with all kinds of s-words for it.

"Sensational. Sexy. Satisfying." When he grinned at her, she couldn't help grinning back. "I guess I went off the theme there."

She picked up her spoon and drifted it through the vegetable soup, watching the chunks swirl in the dark broth. "You couldn't just deny it?"

"Since the source was most likely somebody very close to your brother and I was standing there with a pretty noticeable bruise on my jaw, I thought that might make the whole thing worse. I didn't want them trying to get a statement from you or digging through our garbage or showing up at Firewall or your job, asking questions."

"You're a hockey player, not a movie star."

"True. But even though you try to ignore hockey, you're a Burke." He paused to grimace dramatically to make her laugh. "Sorry. That's just hard to say. Anyway, Burke and I make headlines on the ice. This would definitely make headlines because they'll get site traffic out of it, even if we're not plastered on tabloid covers. It might be on a smaller scale, but how much coverage would it take to get back to your boss?"

"Not a lot," she muttered.

"So I figure your boss might not be super impressed you're dating a professional athlete, but at least you're dating him and didn't just drag him back to your apartment for one night of the best sex of his life."

Hers too, though she wasn't in the mood to stroke his ego or any other part of him right now. He was right about her boss. Stan wouldn't approve of a hockey player, but as long as she played to misogyny and let him believe she was just trying to get a husband and babies, she might not have to kiss the promotion goodbye.

Her phone chimed, and she pulled it out of her bag. It was from Erik, of course. *What the hell, Kris?*

She sighed and flipped the phone around so Will could see the screen. "I guess the news is out. That didn't take long."

"That's why I *had* to talk to you." He chuckled. "Zach might have nightmares for a while, but I didn't actually threaten him. Just so you know."

"I wonder if Dad knows yet. I'm guessing he doesn't or he'd be blowing up my phone but...holy shit, he's going to be pissed."

She typed in a response to Erik. *I'll explain later. Talk after practice tonight? Until you talk to me, don't say anything to anybody, even Dad. NO COMMENT. I mean it.*

Ok for tonight. Let me know when and where.

"I didn't know what else to do," Will said. "I'm sorry."

She looked across the table and lost herself in his dark

gaze for a moment. He was sincere, she knew that. And his first instinct when ambushed by a reporter hadn't been to thump his chest or trash-talk his rival. It had been to protect her and the thing she'd told him was important to her.

"I can handle my dad," she said. "It won't be easy."

"What are you going to tell him? The truth?"

"Ah, that would be a definite *no*. I'll tell him what we'll tell anybody else who asks. We're dating. And I'll probably let Erik believe it, too. His mouth got us into this, and the more people who know a secret, the faster it becomes anything *but* a secret."

"And you think he'll suddenly be okay with us dating?" His voice was heavy with skepticism, which made sense considering they'd spent years hating each other.

"For me? Yes. He won't like it, but once the shock wears off, he'll try to respect my boundaries where you're concerned."

"Okay. I *am* really sorry about this, Kristen."

"You don't have anything to be sorry for." She shrugged. "And I was planning to go to Firewall tonight. If you were there, you were coming home with me again, anyway. I guess I wasn't done with you."

"I was going home with you again, huh? Just like that?"

She extended her leg just enough to brush the inside of his calf and make him jump a little. "Would you have told me you had other plans?"

"Hell no." He shook his head, chuckling. "Dating Erik Burke's sister."

"Fake dating," she said, just to be clear.

"With benefits," he added, with a look that raised the temperature in the restaurant at least ten degrees.

"Fake dating with benefits, until this mess blows over."

Maybe she'd have gotten her fill of him by then.

5

K risten didn't want Will walking her to the front door of her office building, so he was forced to say goodbye to her outside of the restaurant and watch her walk away. Not that he minded the view, but he would have preferred to escort her back to work.

In part because he was a gentleman, but mostly because it would have given him a few more minutes with her.

The first text message arrived a few minutes after he slid into the backseat of an Uber back to his hotel. It buzzed twice more in the time it took him to get the phone out of his pocket to respond to the first message.

Clearly the news had broken in Baltimore.

He ignored the other two and pulled up the first because Mitchell was not only his teammate but had become his closest friend in Baltimore. They'd been picked up by the Harriers a year apart and been inseparable since.

WTF R U doing? A few seconds later, a follow-up message appeared. *EB's sis? DUDE.*

It's a long story.

U been there like a week. How long can it B?

It was a valid point, and Will stared out the window for a few seconds while he considered his response.

The problem was the promise he'd made to Kristen. They weren't going to tell anybody the truth. It had sounded simple enough at the time, but every member of the Harriers organization knew how long he'd been in Boston. While most of them might buy the lie that he and Kristen had been seeing each other in secret because of just this situation, Mitchell wouldn't. He'd be the one guy Will would have confided in.

I'm in an Uber. Typing on the tiny keyboard was a pain in the ass, and it certainly wasn't a conversation he wanted to use dictation for with the driver a foot away. *I'll call you later.*

He wasn't sure what he would tell him, but at least he'd bought a little time to come up with something.

When the car pulled up in front of the hotel Will was temporarily calling home, the driver made eye contact with him in the mirror and smiled. "A nice tip would go a long way toward healing that broken heart you guys gave me in twenty-fifteen."

Will laughed. "I'd apologize, but...you know."

The Harriers had not only brought the Stanley Cup home that year, but they'd had the pleasure of being the team that knocked the Marauders out of contention. He did tip the guy very well, though, but more because he'd been cool about having Cross Lecroix in the backseat of his Hyundai and had neither talked his ear off about the sport nor dumped him off on the side of the road in the cold.

Will had just engaged the security bar on his door and was in the process of taking a deep breath when his phone vibrated again, but this time with a call. And when his dad's name showed up on the screen, he leaned his head against the wall for a few seconds before answering.

Apparently the news had reached Ontario, too.

"Hey, Pop," he said, giving in to the inevitable. Some people could be put off, but not his dad.

"Jesus Murphy, kid. So many people have called me in the last hour, I thought I'd won the lottery."

Will winced. "I should have called you first, but it got hectic here."

"I would have waited, but your mother wants to know if your face is okay and if you put ice on it right away."

"Of course I did." Frozen Brussels sprouts were close enough. "How close is she right now?"

"I can feel her breath on the back of my neck," his dad said, and his words were followed by an annoyed sound from his mother and a chuckle from his father. "I tried to call while she was digging around for her passport and thought it was safe when she dumped an entire file box on the floor, but she caught me."

"I'm okay, Mom." It didn't matter that he wasn't on speakerphone. His dad always had the volume jacked up so high, everybody in the room could hear both sides of any conversation he had.

"How long have you been seeing this girl?" she demanded.

"Not long. It's kind of a recent thing." It was vague, but also not a lie, so he tried to keep the conversation moving before she could try to pin down more details. "You don't need your passport, Mom."

"The hell I don't," she snapped, and he had absolutely no trouble hearing her. "When I have to find out from your father who found out from Donny Jacobs who found out from the internet of all places that my son not only got in a fight—*off* the ice—but has been dating Erik Burke's sister without telling us, I am absolutely going to find my passport."

Will closed his eyes, imagining his mother and his younger sister showing up in Boston to check up on him. "I swear *Hometown Hoser* made it sound like a much bigger deal than it really is. Kristen and I are casually dating, and her brother and I had a bit of a communication issue that's been resolved."

"You couldn't get a date with a woman who's *not* Erik Burke's sister?"

"Mom." He didn't roll his eyes because history lent some validity to the idea she would hear it in his voice. "I didn't know who she was when I first met her. It's just not that big a deal."

"So you've said."

"Didn't you put your passport in your jewelry box so you wouldn't lose it?" he heard his dad say, and then after a few seconds, he spoke to Will again. "That'll buy us five minutes, tops. This is quite a situation you've gotten yourself into, son."

"Yeah, it's a beaut." He wanted to keep talking and just tell his dad the entire truth of the matter because that's what he did. When he had something on his mind, he talked it through with his dad.

But if there was one thing Jack Lecroix wouldn't do, it was keep secrets about their children from his wife, and the truth of what was going on between Will and Kristen would be even harder for her to wrap her mind around than what she thought was happening. Not telling anybody was the right decision, no matter how hard it was.

"I need you to convince Mom to relax, which I know is asking a lot. But that sports journalist made it sound like there's a lot more to it, and other bloggers will pick it up and

probably embellish a little. The truth is pretty boring."
Okay, *that* was a lie, and he felt bad about it. Spending time
with Kristen was anything but boring.

"I'll do my best, but you just make sure you don't put this
woman in a tough position."

"Trust me, Dad, I'm doing everything I can to keep her
from getting caught up in a mess. And my mother and sister
showing up won't help this die down, so if Mom does
manage to find her passport, do me a favor and hide it
again? Along with Cassie's?"

"I'll do my best. Now talk to me about your shoulder.
Any problems?"

While giving his dad an update that was pretty positive,
Will pulled his iPad off its charger and opened the mail app
tied to the email he only used with his professional contacts.
There were already several emails from the PR office, as well
as a few names that made him wince. Pretty much everybody wanted answers, from the top office down.

And he'd answer them at some point, but he read his
contracts pretty closely before he signed them and there
were no clauses giving the Harriers an opinion on who he
dated.

"I found it," Will heard his mother say over his father
asking about the Skimmers' practice facility, and both men
groaned. "Let me talk to him for a minute, Jack."

It took a solid five minutes for Will to convince his mom
there was nothing going on that merited her getting on a
plane to the US. Then he capped off the conversation by
asking about his four-year-old nephew. Talking about her
grandson was always the perfect distraction.

Once the call ended, he plugged his phone in to charge
and sat at the desk with the iPad. After responding to the
emails from PR—making it very clear he didn't want to hear

anything but "no comment" from the Harriers or Skimmers —he sent an email to his social media manager. There was going to be a flood of ugliness, and they were going to ignore it, as usual. But attacks on Kristen wouldn't be tolerated, and those comments should be deleted on platforms that allowed it and the accounts blocked whenever possible. He'd been in the sports corner of the internet long enough to know it wouldn't be pretty, and not only were they trying not to antagonize Kristen's boss, but it would be best for everybody if Will didn't read any comments for a while. He couldn't fight everybody.

With that task out of the way, he killed twenty minutes putting away the clothes the laundry service had delivered and making a list of things he was running short on in the kitchenette. Once he knew Mitchell and the rest of the team would be back on the ice, he called his friend's number and left a voicemail, giving him the same story he'd given his parents. Casually seeing each other. Miscommunication with Burke. Nothing to see here.

Best case scenario, they'd play phone tag for a few days, until it all died down.

But when he finally went to the *Hometown Hoser* site to see for himself, he knew it might take more than a few days for it to fade away. Joel had really missed his calling writing tabloid trash because while he didn't technically change the facts, he made the scandal sound a hell of a lot juicier than it actually was. And a quick Google search told him other sites were picking up the story and running with it. He didn't even bother checking Facebook or Twitter, since it wouldn't do anything but jack up his blood pressure and make it harder to stick to the strict no-comment strategy.

All he could do was hope being Erik Burke's sister would shield Kristen from the more disgusting comments, and that hockey fandom would focus more on the punch in the face than the reason for it.

And that Kristen's conversations with her brother and father didn't blow everything up. He'd wanted to be with her, but she'd made it clear his presence wasn't going to help, so he put on a movie and did his best not to think about it.

KRISTEN DECIDED on drinks at her place rather than meeting her brother in a restaurant or bar for the conversation ahead of them. Not that Erik would cause an unpleasant scene, but because at least one person in any public space tended to recognize him, and she was going to be talking about her sex life.

She'd also refused Will's offer to be present when she explained the situation to Erik, for obvious reasons. They weren't even twenty-four hours from Erik punching Will in the face and that was *before* the situation went publicly sideways. She could reason with her brother, but not if the two men were facing off in some kind of dick-swinging contest.

Erik not only sent her a text message when he arrived at her building, but he knocked on the door and waited for her to let him in. He was still tense, and his mouth was pressed into a tight line, but at least he'd gotten that message.

"Have a seat," she said, gesturing to the two fresh drinks she'd set on the coffee table when she got his text.

He sat in the armchair, as always, but he didn't reach for the glass. "What's going on, Kris? I've been dodging Joel from *Hometown Hoser* and a couple other guys since that post about you and Lecroix being a couple went live."

"That's a stupid name for a site, even if it is about hockey, and what's going on is Will getting ambushed with questions he couldn't get around answering." Somehow that information had come from her brother, which she couldn't forget. When he looked confused, she sighed. "Will is his actual name, you know. His mother didn't name him Cross."

"Oh, yeah. I think I knew that. But the last time we had dinner, you told me you weren't dating anybody. Did you really think you could hide this from me?" When he looked her in the eye, it wasn't anger she saw there. Her brother was hurt, and her face flushed with guilt. "How can you be in a relationship with this guy and not tell me?"

If he'd raged at her, she probably would have stuck to her original plan, which was to lie to him and to let him continue believing what Will had said was the truth. But when everything else was stripped away—the hockey and the resentments and their relationships with their father— Erik was her brother and believing that she'd been seeing Will behind his back would hurt him.

"We don't have a relationship, Erik."

"You sure as hell have something."

"I picked him up in a bar. I didn't know who he was, but I watched him for a while and then I brought him home with me. That was supposed to be the end of it."

His brows drew together, and he shook his head. "Then why the hell did he tell that reporter you've been dating?"

"Because somebody ran their mouth about last night. It wasn't me and it wasn't Will, so..." She let the accusation go unsaid, one eyebrow arched.

"I went out with a couple of the guys after. Had a few drinks." He sighed and leaned back in his chair. "I was pissed, so I might have said some shit."

"Yeah, and one of those guys you went out with told somebody else who thought it would be a cool story for the sports page." She felt herself getting heated and forced herself to calm down. "Or you were talking loud enough that somebody else overheard you."

"I'm sorry, Kris. I'm going to find out if it was one of the guys I was with because they were Marauders, and if one of them ran his mouth about you...I'll find out, I promise."

"Will had a split second to consider the fact the real story could cost me my promotion. That me picking up your biggest rival in a bar for a one-night stand could be a juicy enough story that the mainstream media might pick it up."

"And you guys dating *won't* be a story?" He leaned forward and picked up his drink, downing half of it in one shot. Hers was almost empty, so she didn't blame him a bit.

She inhaled slowly through her nose before the blowing the breath out through her mouth. She wasn't sure she'd be able to make him understand. "It's a story no matter what. But one version paints a picture of a woman falling for her brother's professional opponent in some kind of star-crossed romance or some shit. The other version stars a woman looking for a one-night stand in a bar. You know how people get—how guys like my boss get—when it comes to women who just want to get laid."

"I...shit."

Kristen chuckled softly. "You're trying so hard not to put your hands over your ears and sing *la la la, I can't hear you* right now."

"I do *not* want to talk about your sex life."

"Trust me, I don't want to be talking about it, either. But you not only punched Will in the face, you then ranted about it to your buddies. I don't know if it was one of them or just some asshole within earshot, but somebody put my personal business on blast, and here we are."

"So it was just a one-night stand?"

"It was probably going to be a few nights, actually." When he groaned, she laughed. "I'll spare you the details, but you know how I feel about the sport. You really think, after all this time being a hockey sister, I'd sign on to be a hockey wife?"

"I'm sorry I might blow up your promotion, Kris. I really am. But what am I supposed to do now? Smile and tell the world I'm thrilled my sister is dating Cross Lecroix?"

"You can't even bluff your way through a round of poker, so there's no way you'd pull that off. You don't have to give us your blessing or anything. Just tell anybody who asks that my personal life is my business and you wish me the best."

"They'll still talk. Your boss will probably still hear some of it." When she opened her mouth to respond, he held up his hand. "No, I get it. As long as your boss thinks you're in a proper *courtship* or whatever, he won't have a problem with it."

"I'm not sure he'll approve of a professional hockey player, but yeah. Basically, that's the situation. You owe me this, Erik. I've lived in your shadow my entire life, and now I have a chance to take a big step forward in my career. If you don't go along with this, I could lose my promotion."

"I'm going to do whatever you need to do, but I still think he's using you to hurt me."

Her temper rose, and she clenched her hands into fists. "This isn't about you. I told you last night that, contrary to our father's opinion, not everything is. Will didn't know I was your sister when we hooked up."

"So he says." Concern for her softened the hard lines of his face. "I mean, what are the chances?"

Kristen remembered the look on Will's face when he realized he was naked in the bed of Erik Burke's sister. It had been nothing short of horror, and there was a good chance

Erik would never believe it was a weird coincidence in a small world, but she did.

"Believe whatever you want," she said rather than waste time trying to convince him. "I don't care. The only thing I care about is you swearing to me that you won't contradict what Will told the press to anybody. Even Dad."

"You want me to lie to *Dad*?"

Erik was a lot closer to Lamont than Kristen was. It was just the natural order of things in the Burke family, and she'd accepted it years ago. But she also knew Erik loved her, and if she could get him to make this promise to her, he wouldn't break it. Not even for their father.

"Let me ask you this," she said, leaning back in her chair. "Which do you think is more important to Dad—my career and promotion or denying anybody in the Burke family could ever be involved in any way with Cross Lecroix?"

"He'd throw you under the bus if it got him sports media time," he admitted with obvious reluctance. "I'm sorry, because even though you and I both know it's true, I hate saying it out loud."

"I know, but it is what it is, so I need you to promise you won't tell *anybody* the actual truth about me and Will. Please."

"I'll do it. I won't even tell Dad." She kept looking at him until he chuckled. "I promise."

"Thank you."

"Have you heard from him yet? I was expecting him to blow up my phone, but he doesn't like to distract me from ice time, so it should be coming anytime now."

She rolled her eyes. "I haven't spoken to him, but I got a text message demanding I be available for a phone call at six o'clock."

Erik tapped his phone screen to see the time and then

grinned. "Oh, look at the time. I just remembered I have a thing I'm supposed to be doing in five minutes."

"Chicken," she teased, and she got up to put their empty glasses in the sink while he put his coat on.

"I'm sorry about all this," he said sincerely, wrapping his arms around her for a brief hug. "I lost my shit when I saw him in your bedroom, but the rest of it...I would never do anything to hurt you, Kris. I'm really sorry."

"I know. This'll pass and eventually it'll just be a funny *hey, remember that one time* story we tell when Dad isn't around."

He laughed and kissed her cheek. "I'd tell you to let me know how the conversation with Dad goes, but I'm pretty sure I'll hear all about it."

"No doubt."

He paused in the doorway. "None of that apology is for Cross, though. Just to be clear. I'm not sorry I got that shot in at all."

"I figured as much." The shrill sound of her phone's ringer echoed through the apartment, and she cringed.

"Hey, gotta go," Erik said, and then he fled, pulling the door closed behind him.

When she picked up the phone and saw *Dad* on the screen, she thought about sending him to voicemail. She wasn't in the mood for Lamont Burke tonight. But he'd warned her this call was coming and dodging it would escalate things. He might even show up at her door. "Hello?"

"What the hell are you thinking?"

"Hi, Pop. How are you? I'm fine, thanks." Not that this call was any different from his calls in the past. Since most of his communications revolved around her brother, he often forgot to make even a token effort to show an interest in her life.

"Don't give me your attitude today, when you're making a mess of your brother's career."

She wanted to laugh out loud at her dad's melodrama, but he had limits and her being amused by this situation would definitely go too far. He didn't have a sense of humor when it came to hockey. "Erik's career seems to be just fine."

"It won't be if he's focusing on you and this stunt you're pulling instead of on his game."

Kristen closed her eyes, pinching the bride of her nose. She was tired of it—tired of *him*—and just really tired in general. She should have let him rant to her voicemail box until the system cut him off.

It was too late for that, though, so she took a deep breath and decided to once again try to placate him instead of telling him to mind his own damn business. He considered everything even tangentially related to Erik his business, so she'd end up backed into a corner where her only option was to tell him to fuck off. She wasn't ready to do that yet.

Maybe she wouldn't ever be. Every time the words formed in her brain, begging to be unleashed, she thought about the fact that cutting her father out of her life permanently would mean having no parents at all. She'd lost her mother, but as long as she accepted Lamont was the way he was, she still had her dad. And turning her back on her dad would put a strain on her relationship with Erik. Not that it would come between them—nothing would ever do that— but it would make seeing each other a lot harder.

So she never said the words, even when he was being like this. And she wouldn't say them now. "I'm not pulling a stunt, Pop, and Erik and I have discussed this already."

"And did it ever occur to you that you should discuss it with *me*?"

She snorted in disbelief before her filter could catch up.

Talk about her sex life with her father? Not likely. She'd had to ask a neighbor lady to help her make her first gynecological appointment because the grown man in the house had literally put his hands over his ears and shouted for her to stop talking to him about that inappropriate shit.

It was the last time she'd ever attempted to talk to him about anything even tangentially related to her vagina.

"Are you acting out?" he demanded. "You're jealous of the attention your brother gets, so you're going to embarrass him like this?"

Kristen pulled the phone away from her ear, and her thumb hovered over the red circle that would end the call. It wouldn't be as satisfying as throwing the phone against the wall, but she knew she'd regret that kind of outburst later when she didn't have a cell phone and had to jump through the hoops to get a replacement.

Lamont was a toxic cloud in her life. She knew it, but as long as his cloud wasn't actively blocking her sunshine, she rolled with it. Better a dad who was kind of an asshole than no dad, she guessed. But every once in a while, that cloud would drop down like a toxic funnel cloud and batter her emotional shutters.

But he had a tendency to get pretty ugly when she hung up on him and, while she wasn't afraid of him, she didn't feel like a pissed off Lamont Burke talking to the press was going to do any of them any favors.

"This has nothing to do with Erik," she said calmly. "I met a guy, and we hit it off. His name is Will, and it turns out they call him Cross professionally, but I didn't know that at the time."

"How long has this been going on?"

Okay, *that* was a problem. If they were going to lie to everybody, they probably should have spent a few minutes on their cover story. The when they met and how they met details would probably trip them up.

"A while," she said, opting against specifics. And then, knowing her dad in a temper would follow the bouncing rage ball, she turned the conversation away from the details she didn't have. "He's a really great guy, Dad."

It sounded as if he choked on something—maybe his beloved bourbon—and she winced. Having to call an ambulance for her dad because her so-called relationship with Will almost killed him would do the opposite of making the story boring.

"He's an asshole," Lamont barked, and Kristen was relieved. If he could bark, he could breathe. Actually, with him it was more like, if he was breathing, he was barking.

"But just imagine what amazing hockey players our sons would be," she snapped, even though the idea of her having kids any time soon, especially with a hockey player she accidentally picked up in a bar, was ridiculous.

When Lamont didn't say anything, she wondered if he'd been struck speechless with horror at the thought of a Lecroix grandchild or if he was actually thinking about the potential talent—and marketability—of a kid with Burke and Lecroix DNA.

"This is how it is," she finally said in a firm voice, wanting to put an end to the nonsense. "If everybody keeps their mouths shut beyond what's already been said, and you and Erik don't say anything except that my personal life is my own business, everybody gets bored and moves on. The only way this stays a story is if *you* make it a story, and then any distraction from Erik's game is also on you."

"The fastest way to make the story go away is for you to break things off with Lecroix," Lamont countered.

He had a point. It would be easy to say that, after the

news broke, they'd decided it would be too much and went their separate ways. End of story.

But she didn't really know how long Will would be in Boston, and as long as he was in this city, she wasn't sure she'd be able to resist him. And maybe a breakup would be just as newsworthy as dating, if not more, because it would look like Erik punching Will had caused it, which could get everybody excited about an increase in the animosity between the two men. It was better for everybody to let the story ride for a while.

"That's not your decision to make," she said.

"We should be focusing on the All-Star weekend, not on your nonsense."

That was nothing new. "Then stop arguing with me and go watch game tapes or something. You've never let anything going on in my life detract from game prep before, so there's no sense in starting now."

He grunted and hung up, which was how their phone calls usually ended. She sank onto the couch and closed her eyes, blowing out a long breath.

Dealing with Erik and her dad in the same day was always tiring, but tonight she felt absolutely drained. A lot had happened today, and she still had tomorrow to look forward to. If her boss was going to hear what had happened, it would probably be before she showed up to work in the morning. She was hopeful the dating angle would be enough to make Stan dismiss it all, but Will was still an athlete. And not only was he a hockey player, but he was the one the people of Boston hated the most.

All she wanted to do for the rest of the night was binge some Netflix and then fall into her bed, even though she'd probably do more tossing and turning, tangling her sheets all up, than actual sleeping. She'd worry about tomorrow when her alarm went off.

Her phone chimed, and she caught herself smiling when Will's name popped up on the screen.

Since we're dating now, do you want to grab some grilled chicken with me?

Netflix wasn't going anywhere, she decided. And if she was going to spend a sleepless night in tangled sheets, it might as well be Will who tangled them.

6

W ill watched Kristen walk through the door of Firewall, just as he had the first time he'd eaten there, and the impact of her gaze meeting his wasn't lessened any by having been naked in her bed.

If anything, his hunger for her hit him even harder.

He'd had a few relationships in his life—a couple of them he'd really believed at the time would go the distance —but he'd never been as excited by a woman as he was by this one. She was not only sexy as hell, but she was funny and authentic and pretty damn fierce.

She was also a Burke, but nobody was perfect.

He stood when she reached the table, and she gave him a quick but potent kiss, complete with a sharp nip at his bottom lip, before she sat in the chair across from his. Sitting helped stop his erection before it could become a problem, but he figured he'd better get used to constantly being semihard if he was going to be spending a lot of time with Kristen.

"I'm surprised you don't hang out at sports bars," she said. "You'd probably eat—or at least drink—for free."

He snorted at the suggestion. "I think you're seriously underestimating how much this city loves your brother. You said yourself I was in the top three most hated athletes in Boston on a good day, and now Marauders fans know I did, in fact, defile Burke's sister."

"Thoroughly defiled," she said, amusement making her eyes crinkle. "But whether they hate you or not, fans aren't going to pass up the chance to have a story to tell about the time they had a drink with Cross Lecroix."

"I'd rather eat my dinner and read my book in peace. Autographs and selfies come with being at the top of my game, but I get time off, too."

She propped her chin on her hand. "Does that mean I can't ask you for an autograph?"

He laughed. "I guess that depends on where you want me to sign my name."

"Tell me you've never signed a breast." He felt the heat in his face and knew he didn't even have to answer. She rolled her eyes. "You're not writing your name on my body. But I do think it would be hilarious to have you sign a Cross Lecroix poster so I can hang it in my apartment. Cross as Dad repellent would be pretty effective."

"The way you say that makes me wonder if you think of me and Cross Lecroix as two different people in your head." She shrugged and didn't deny it. "We're not. If anything, Cross is the real me. Will's the guy hanging out in Boston waiting for the clock to tick down on the All-Star break and his conditioning stint so he can get back on the ice in Baltimore."

"So noted." The seriousness in her gaze told him she'd got what he was trying to say without actually saying it. This was a short, involuntary detour in his life, and she shouldn't think it was anything else. Then the corner of her mouth turned up suggestively. "Of course, Will's also the guy having sex with me while that clock ticks."

"It *is* good to be Will right now," he admitted, and his dick twitched to life again.

"Let's stop talking about you in dual third-person and order food," she suggested, which worked for him. Talking about sex while they weren't in a place they could actually have it was going to make for a very long, uncomfortable evening.

And it had been a difficult enough day already. Since the news about Kristen broke, he'd been hearing from pretty much everybody he had a professional connection to—from the Harriers management to his agent and his own teammates—as well as getting text messages from a lot of guys he had friendships with off the ice. It had been exhausting and one of the perks of dinner with Kristen was being with somebody who actually knew the truth.

But the biggest benefit was the way he felt when she turned her gaze on him and her half smile seemed to promise good things. And not just sex—though he certainly wouldn't turn it down—but just the pleasure of her company. He liked her with her clothes on, too.

"So, how many panicked or irate phone calls have you gotten?" she asked after they'd put in their order.

"Let's just say I've had to charge my phone twice already today. But none of the people who called me were Lamont Burke, so I have that going for me."

She laughed and nodded. "Yes, you do. Have I mentioned you're buying tonight?"

"Sounds fair. Was it as bad as I imagine it was?"

"He didn't actually show up at my door, so it could have

been worse. But, no, it wasn't pleasant. He accused me of trying to get attention because I'm jealous of Erik."

The happy glow he'd been working on was swept away by a rush of anger, and Will set down his glass so he didn't crack it. "I think I probably shouldn't tell you how I feel about that because the bottom line is that he's your father."

"I'm used to it," she said with a shrug.

"That doesn't make it better. It's worse, actually. This kind of shit would be bad enough as a one-time deal, but it's not. You shouldn't *have* to be used to it."

"Shh." She reached across the table and laced her fingers through his. "You're getting loud, and you're going to attract attention, and we're here because you *don't* attract attention, so if you cause a scene, you'll be eating shitty grilled chicken someplace else. And I know I shouldn't have to be used to my dad being a dick, but I am. But I also know I can't change him, so it is what it is."

"What about Burke?" He winced. "Your brother, I mean. You're all Burkes, I guess."

"Erik can't change him, either." She let go of his hand to pick up her drink. "He's not like Dad, you know. He was raised to be the center of our universe, but he does his best to never leave me behind. We're very close, even when Dad makes it hard."

The last thing Will wanted to do right now was talk about the Burke men—and he especially didn't want to hear praise for the guy he'd been battling for a decade and a half —so he decided a change of subject was in order. "Since you know a hell of a lot about my job, why don't you tell me about yours? And this promotion you want?"

She grimaced. "I basically manage a very large office for an asshole I definitely don't want to talk about, or even think about, right now."

"Okay. Favorite color?"

"Red." She chuckled. "Yours?"

"Blue." Yesterday, he probably would have said he didn't have one. But now that he'd seen her eyes, it was definitely blue. But he wasn't quite ready to give up on talking about *her* yet. "Okay, I hate pushing, and I know I shouldn't, but you're such a strong, confident woman and I get why you might put up with your dad being a jerk, but putting up with an asshole boss doesn't seem like you."

"I took the job because it was available, paid enough to cover my student loans *and* food, and fit my career plan. Plus, my boss is well-respected in the city. You don't know until you work in a place what really happens in the office, you know?"

"But you've stayed."

"He's going to run for mayor, and he's probably going to win. And because I've stuck it out and worked my ass off, I'm going to be the chief of staff for the mayor of Boston. And with *that* on my resume, instead of job-hopping for less money because I don't personally like my boss, I'm going to use his connections and my skills to make a lateral or forward move to campaign manager or chief of staff for somebody I *do* like." She shrugged and took a sip of her drink. "He's a stepping stone for me."

"And a judgmental prick."

"One I'll be happy to leave behind, but not until the time is right for me. And now I *really* don't want to think about him anymore."

"Okay, what's your favorite movie, then?"

"*Misery.*"

"Horror?" That surprised him. Hell, *everything* about her surprised him. "I'm partial to horror myself, both in books and movies."

They talked for two hours about the horror books and movies they both liked, then moved on to others. And then television shows. They talked about pretty much everything *but* their families and hockey. She had several cocktails, while he stuck to ice water and his decaf, and they split a strawberry shortcake for dessert.

"You didn't drive here, did you?" he asked when she was halfway through her third drink.

"Nope. After the day I had, I decided to take a Lyft so I wouldn't have to be conflicted about a second drink." She lifted the glass. "Or a third. Did I not mention you're driving me home?"

He chuckled and clinked his coffee mug lightly against her glass. "It'll be my pleasure."

"Probably." Her expression said his chances at pleasure were higher than *probably*, but he wouldn't push her. After the day they'd both had, he would totally understand if she just wanted to climb into her bed alone and pull the covers up over her head.

It wouldn't sound like a bad plan to him, either, if he hadn't been in various states of semi-erect from the minute she walked through the door. Whether Kristen invited him in or he had to have some solo time in his hotel shower, his dick was going to need a little attention before he could sleep.

The first thing she did when they got in his car was change the radio station. He'd been listening to sports radio, mostly to get an overview of how the day in sports in general had gone. But, of course, they were talking hockey when he fired up the ignition.

"Things are getting interesting in the Boston hockey scene," was the first thing they heard, and she hit the scan button before they heard more.

"Let's just pretend they were going to talk about the Zamboni or something," she said, scanning until she found a song she liked.

As he drove, Kristen sang along to the radio with the confidence and enthusiasm of somebody who'd consumed three fairly strong cocktails, and he enjoyed it immensely. She wasn't drunk, by any means, but she was definitely more relaxed than she'd been when she walked into Firewall.

When he pulled into a spot just down the street from her building, she unbuckled her seatbelt and turned to him. "You coming up?"

"I'm definitely walking you to the door. But as for coming up, are you sure want me to?"

She shrugged. "If I have to fake date you, I may as well get some great sex out of it."

"That's a weird combination of very flattering, and yet somehow not."

"Maybe just focus on the great sex part."

He could do that. "I'm definitely coming up, then."

THE NEXT MORNING, it was nothing short of a miracle that Kristen managed to get to work on time. She was exhausted and sore—though in the best possible way—and she definitely didn't look her best. But she wasn't late.

Annie, who was the head of HR as well as her friend, poked her head in the door within a minute of her arrival. "Stan's looking for you."

Kristen looked at her watch. "It's not time for our morning meeting yet."

"I don't think it's that. He seems agitated, and he asked

about you first thing, and he's asked about every two minutes if you're here yet."

She sighed. So he knew. It was surprising he hadn't called her cell phone, despite his preference for face-to-face meetings. "Thanks for the heads-up."

As tempting as it was to wait until their usual meeting time or to simply ignore the summons, Kristen decided there was no sense in putting it off. She walked down the short hall to Stan's office.

The door was open, so she knocked on the jamb. "You wanted to see me?"

He looked up from his computer screen. "Kristen, come in. Close the door behind you, please."

She did as she was told and then sat in her usual chair with her hands folded in her lap.

"It's been brought to my attention that you had some kind of a domestic situation that unfortunately made headlines yesterday."

It was hard to keep a straight face—she couldn't sneer at his uptight tone *or* laugh at his melodrama, nor could she let her extreme annoyance show—but she mentally repeated the word *promotion* to keep herself in check. "I don't think a sports blog qualifies as 'making headlines,' but yes, there was some interest in my personal life."

"You are aware, of course, that your actions reflect on me and this office, right?"

Only if you're a self-absorbed misogynist. "It was a misunderstanding, Stan. I'm dating a wonderful man, and my brother was taken by surprise when he found out it was somebody he knew. That's all."

Stan scowled. "The article made it sound far more sordid than that."

"Again, it was a blog post, not an article." It was a ridiculous and irrelevant distinction, but it would matter to him.

"And he's a hockey player, if I read it correctly?"

He knew damn well he'd read it correctly, and he also knew her brother played hockey professionally. Stan hadn't hesitated to use that connection in the past when free tickets to a Marauders game would help him schmooze with people he wanted to impress, so he should watch the hypocrisy. She would only tolerate so much.

"He plays for a Baltimore team, yes." She was about to stress the fact he wouldn't be in Boston long, but then she remembered she was supposed to be selling them as a stable, committed couple. "This shouldn't come up again, Stan. I've spoken to my brother and there shouldn't be any more headlines."

"I hope you're right. I would hate to see you in some kind of scandal that would reflect poorly on this office."

"It won't happen," she assured him again, more firmly this time, while she called him a lot of unsavory names in her head.

The man liked to put on airs as though he were gearing up for a run at the White House instead of the mayor's office. The only thing that reflected poorly on his office was him, but it all happened behind closed office doors, so the city just saw the smiling and successful businessman with the picture-perfect family.

Because she didn't want to delve any deeper into her personal life for Stan, she stood. For a few seconds, he looked like he wanted to say more, but then he gave her the smile he seemed to think was charming but was actually smarmy. "I'm glad to hear it. And it's good that you've found yourself a beau. I'm happy for you, Kristen."

She managed to leave his office and close the door

behind her before the derisive snort escaped. A *beau*? What the hell was that about?

Annie managed to get out of the water cooler conversation she was having in time to meet Kristen at her office door. "Everything okay? You look pissed."

"It's fine. I'm just trying to recover from my journey back to 1955."

"He saw the blog post, didn't he?"

"*You* saw the blog post?" Annie had no interest in sports that Kristen knew of.

Annie blushed. "I think everybody's seen it. I was going to text you yesterday, but my mom called with one of her crises and it got late. I was really hoping Stan wouldn't hear about it, though."

"I was, too, but he probably has Google alerts set up for each of us."

Annie laughed out loud. "I'd say you're probably right, except he can barely check his own email without calling the IT guy for help. I have to run, but we're having lunch together today because I want to hear more about this Cross guy."

Kristen didn't have long before she'd have to go back into Stan's office for their regular morning meeting, so she excused herself and closed her door against the office chatter—a lot of which was probably about her.

She sat at her desk and went through her usual post-Stan ritual, which included some deep breathing, muttered obscenities, and visualizing herself in the future, working for a better, more powerful, less ignorant and much less conservative boss.

At least he seemed mollified by the fact Will was her *beau*. She had a nasty feeling that meeting would have gone in a totally unpleasant direction if he knew the true story—

her one-night stand with the hot guy she picked up at a bar had ended with her brother punching him in the face.

She made it through the rest of the day without any further mention of the incident other than giving Annie the more fun details of the story over salads—skirting over the details about how it all got started, and focusing instead on how great a guy Will was—and Stan seemed to be his usual self, returning to normal levels of being insufferable.

This is good, she told herself as she made her way home. Will's bruise would fade. She was cautiously optimistic her promotion was still on track. And she was having the best sex of her life in the meantime. Considering the potential for disaster that had existed, things were going pretty damn well.

Her apartment felt a little empty without Will in it, though, and she couldn't stop herself from thinking about him as she sorted her mail—dumping most of it in the recycling tub—and changed into leggings and a sweatshirt. She was feeling antsy, so she picked up her phone and sent Will a text message.

I feel like going for a drive. Wanna go with?

If you can wait an hour. Finishing up and need to shower. Meet at practice facility?

She'd rather not be anywhere near the place, but she also didn't want to wait any longer than she had to before she got to see him. *Give me the address and I'll be there in an hour.*

He sent it, and she saved it to her navigation so she could pull it up when it was time. Then, with a little time to kill, she pulled up the schedule Erik sent her every week and decided now might be a good time to catch him.

He answered on the third ring. "Hey, Kris. How are things?"

"Strange and somewhat hard to believe. How are things with you?"

"About the same." She could tell by the sound quality and ambient noise that he was driving, and she put him on speakerphone so she could clean her bathroom while she talked to him. "Things are weird, for sure. I'm taking a lot of shit about this from the team, as you can imagine."

"Maybe choose more discreet friends to vent to in the future."

"No shit, and again, I'm sorry about that. But hopefully it'll all blow over soon, especially for you. In the locker room, somebody's always giving somebody shit for something, and it's just my turn until something more interesting happens." He chuckled. "It's a pretty high bar, though."

"We Burkes don't do anything halfway."

"No, we don't. How's Cross handling it?"

"He's good. Everybody blew up his phone yesterday, of course, but he stuck with the story, refused to say anything more, and I think people are getting bored already."

"Have you seen him since...you know?"

"Yeah, we've spent some time together." She didn't really want to give any more details than that, and she guessed he didn't want to hear them because he didn't ask.

"You're okay, though? At work and stuff? Because that's all that really matters."

"I'm good. And Stan did hear about it all, of course, but it didn't bother him as much when I told him Will and I are dating. He said he was happy I found—and get this—a *beau*."

Erik's laughter filled her bathroom. "Are you serious? Did he actually use that word?"

"He did. I was surprised he didn't tell me I should start wearing corsets and hoop skirts to the office from now on."

"He's such a jerk," he said, sounding less amused now. "I hate that you work for somebody like that."

"I know, but like I've told you a hundred times, he's a means to an end. I can put up with him for now."

They chatted a few more minutes, and then Kristen told him she had to let him go. She didn't tell him why, but she could tell by his voice that he'd guessed why. It was a good thing she and Will were only fake dating because bringing him to family dinners would make Thanksgiving awkward for a good long time.

She pulled into the lot for the Skimmers' practice facility about five minutes later than she'd intended to, and she spotted Will right away. He was freshly showered and leaning against a light post with his hockey bag slung over his shoulder.

When he saw her, he lifted his hand in a wave and then walked to the curb. She lowered the passenger side window, and he leaned down to speak to her.

"Where's your car?" she asked, since the parking lot was pretty empty and she didn't see his rental.

"At the hotel I'm staying in. It's close enough to walk, and it wasn't too cold today."

She hit the button to pop the trunk. "Throw your bag in and let's go, then."

He hesitated. "Do you want me to drive?"

She wasn't even surprised by the question. "Do I want you to drive my car around my city? Not really."

"Hey, you can save on gas if we go grab my rental and take that."

She laughed at him before shaking her head. "Nope. If you can't handle the passenger seat with a woman behind the wheel, you can walk back to your hotel. Alone."

"Of course I can handle it," he said, rallying when she pointed out he was being ridiculous.

After closing his hockey bag in the trunk, he opened the passenger door. He had to put the seat all the way back before he could get in, and she bit back her amusement at his expression when he closed the door and put his seatbelt on.

He was *not* comfortable in the shotgun seat, and she didn't care if it was because she was a woman or he just liked being in control. She was going to have a little fun with him.

7

Of all the ways he could die, Will had never thought it would be in the passenger seat of a car being driven by a woman who drove like Boston was nothing but a video game and she was navigating a boss level while she laughed at him.

"Stop covering your eyes," she said as she cut the car over a lane, into a space that looked half the length of the actual vehicle. "You're a hockey player, for chrissake. You're supposed to be tougher than this."

"You're a menace." But he put his hands in his lap, clenching his phone to keep from grabbing the dash or the door handle. He hoped he didn't snap the phone in half.

"We'll be there soon."

"Be where? I thought we were just going for a drive. Like a nice *relaxing* drive." He sucked in a breath as she took an exit ramp without slowing down. "Okay, I'm sorry I implied I should do the driving just because I'm a man. We can't help it. It's just how we're wired."

"You can help it. You just don't want to." But she slowed

down and actually used her signal when she made the next turn.

He was quiet for a little while, since there was no good way out of the conversational hole he'd dug for himself. And he was watching as the neighborhoods around them changed as she made her way through congested streets without her nav system. She obviously knew where she was going, even if she didn't tell him their destination.

"How was work today?" he asked after a while. After he said it, he realized he was risking her being pissed off behind the wheel again if her day had gone badly and he brought it up, but he'd been thinking about her all day. And, really, her driving couldn't get much more aggressive. "Your boss, I mean. Did he find out?"

"He did, but I think your plan worked," she said. "I was able to make it sound suitably respectable and kind of threw Erik under the bus since Stan already knew he plays hockey, so his expectation of him is already low."

"Good. I'm glad I'm not costing you your job, at least."

"And how was your day? The shoulder okay?"

"Seems good. I'm pretty limited in practicing with them, and I spend more time in the occupational therapy rooms than on the ice, but I'm on schedule to play after the break."

"Good. I'm glad your shoulder's healing."

She didn't ask him any more questions about it, and he didn't really expect her to. It seemed odd to him that she hated hockey as much as she did, considering her brother played, but there was probably a reason for it. If she wanted to share, she would. But it was slightly limiting, having the one thing that filled his life being something she didn't want to talk about.

"This looks like a good place to park," she said, and he had to admit she parallel parked flawlessly. His mother and sister would both rather walk a mile carrying whatever they bought than parallel park.

"Where are we, exactly?"

She killed the engine and gave him a smile. "You'll see. It's just a short walk from here."

He was glad it was a fairly decent day for January in Boston and, because he'd walked to practice, he had a coat and warm boots. Kristen grabbed her parka from the back-seat, and after getting out of the car, she pulled it on and zipped it up.

Then she took his hand, and they started walking.

Usually Will liked to be in control of his life. Knowing what he was doing, where he was going—as well as why—were things he was accustomed to, and he didn't like being in the dark. But walking down the sidewalk with his fingers laced through Kristen's, he realized he didn't mind so much. He was content to follow wherever she was leading. Especially since it meant she wasn't driving anymore.

"Okay, this is it." She pointed at a small, unassuming house that was obviously very old but also well cared for.

"Oh, no shit," he said as the words on the sign registered. "Abigail Adams was born here?"

"I think the house has been moved a couple of times, but she was born in it and lived in it until she got married. And it's not open this time of year, and it's already getting dark, which sucks, but I figured you could take a picture for your mom. She might think it's kind of cool."

"She'll think it's *very* cool." He pulled his phone out of his pocket to take some pictures, but he paused to smile at her so she'd know he meant it. "Because it is. This is very cool."

"Since you've been reading her biography, you probably know a lot more about her than I do, but I've been by here a few times over the years, so I'd seen the birthplace signs."

He took a few pictures, getting several angles of the house, before he gestured for her to join him. "Let's do the selfie thing."

"Do you hear yourself right now?" she teased, shaking her head.

"Fans are always asking me for selfies, and now I'm asking. I'm a Kristen fan, so get in here."

"A Kristen fan? Really?" She sighed dramatically, but stepped in front of him and was patient while he framed it so their faces and the Abigail Adams birthplace sign on the house were in the shot. Just before he hit the button, he lowered his cheek to the top of her head, and she was smiling when the shutter sound clicked.

"That's a good one," she said, and he agreed. Her blue eyes were sparkling in the photo, and even in a photograph, the warmth of her smile heated his blood.

It was a photo he'd be keeping in the *Favorites* album on his phone for a very long time.

"Thank you for this," he said, hoping she'd hear the depth of sincerity in his voice. "It means a lot to me that you not only remembered what I was reading and that my mom read it, too, but cared enough to bring me out here to get a picture for her."

"It's not like it's a big deal."

"Actually, it is. A lot of people don't bother to pay attention to anything about me other than the hockey. That's all they see."

She grinned and bumped him with her elbow. "I hate hockey, so I guess it's easier for me to see the other things you like."

"Good point."

"The temperature's dropping," she said, shoving her hands deep into her parka's pockets. "We should head back to the car."

Because she had her hands in her pockets, he didn't get to hold her hand on the walk back, but it was okay. She asked him a few questions about Abigail Adams, and they talked about the former First Lady until they were back in her car with the heat on full blast.

"Have you eaten yet?" she asked, glancing over at him. Then she scowled and shook her head once. "Never mind. Forget I asked that."

"Did you forget you already have plans or something?" He hadn't eaten yet, which she could probably figure out since she'd picked him up at the rink.

"No, I just...it's dumb, but I realized I've already monopolized your time. Just because we're having some fun and told the world we're dating doesn't mean we have to actually spend time together. It's not like the paparazzi is hiding in bushes, waiting to take pictures of us together."

"I wouldn't put anything past Joel," he muttered. "He thought he had a much juicier story, and he's probably really bummed right now. But on a serious note, I haven't eaten and there's nobody in this city I'd rather spend time with than you."

Even in the dark interior of her car, he could see the flush across her cheeks in the flashes of streetlights. "What are you in the mood for?"

He chuckled, because he could think of a few things.

"For *dinner*, smart-ass," she said. "We'll talk about dessert later."

"TELL ME ABOUT MOVING TO BOSTON," Will said.

Kristen looked up from the haddock she was squeezing lemon juice over and cocked her head. "What do you mean?"

"I don't know. It's a little weird, I guess, that I know a little bit about you already because of your brother. I know your family's from Michigan, for example. But I don't want to know the stuff that's in his bio. I want to know about *you,* if that makes sense."

"I guess it does, because I felt the same way when I decided not to do a Google search for your name," she said, smiling at him. "Though I have read your hockey bio, of course."

"There's honestly not much more to know than what's in my hockey bio, I guess. Parents and a younger sister and her family in Ontario. Remind me to show you the twenty-thousand or so pictures and videos of my nephew I have on my phone." His face lit up when he talked about his family, and she liked that about him. "His name's Billy because he's named after me, and he's four. Already a bruiser on skates, of course."

She laughed. "Of course he is."

"So, did you move here when your brother did?"

She nodded. "Well, not right away. I stayed with friends to finish high school when Erik signed with the Marauders."

"Because your dad went with him even though you were still in school."

"Stop making that face or people will think you've been sucking on this lemon. But yes, Lamont came to Boston with Erik. I hated being so far away from him—my brother, not my dad—so I applied to Boston colleges, and here I am."

"I'm surprised you and your brother are so close."

She shrugged one shoulder. "We just are. Just like nobody knows the badass Cross Lecroix likes to read biographies and squeals like a guinea pig when in the passenger seat of a car, there's a side of Erik Burke nobody else really gets to see, either."

"Hey, now. I did not squeal like a guinea pig and, even if I did, it was merited. You drive like you were born in this city."

"Thank you," she said, even though he clearly hadn't meant it as a compliment.

"If he got traded, would you have moved?"

That was a tough question. "I don't know. I know I didn't like being half a country away from him, so I would have considered it. But I also fell in love with Boston pretty quickly, so it would have been hard, so let's just be thankful for the Marauders."

"No," he said, and they both laughed.

"You were with a couple of teams before the Harriers, but you've been there a long time. Has your family considered moving to Baltimore?"

He shook his head. "No, because even to me, Baltimore isn't home. I mean, it's a great city, and I've enjoyed living there, but home is home. Throw in the fact it's an entirely different country, and it was never really considered. They come down for big games, though, and stay in a hotel or get an Airbnb near my condo."

"Do you own a house in Canada?"

"No. I live in Baltimore full-time. But I go home a lot, when I can, and I just stay in my old room."

"Tell me it has a twin bed and all your high school trophies on a big bookshelf."

He blushed, which was cute as hell. "The twin bed went away in the remodel, and the shelf of trophies got banished to my dad's den."

He told her about his family while they ate, and she loved how relaxed he looked when he talked about them.

She noticed he kept the conversation away from growing up a hockey player, and talked instead about fishing with his dad and his mother trying to teach him to bake, and how his sister had been better at car maintenance lessons than he was. It was hard, a little bit, to hear and see the love between father and son when he talked about his dad. Obviously she didn't have that relationship with Lamont, but Erik didn't, either. Their father's obsession with making Erik the best didn't leave time for fishing trips or changing the oil in the car. Hell, she didn't even know if her father knew how to fish. She'd never asked him.

"Do you guys want dessert?" the server asked when she appeared to clear their dinner plates, and Kristen smiled as Will's leg slid against hers and he gave her a look that promised a far sweeter dessert than anything they had on the menu.

"I think we'll pass," she replied and was rewarded with a sizzling grin from Will.

They walked hand in hand back to her car, with Will on the street side of the sidewalk, guiding her around puddles of hard slush from the last time it snowed. He was such a gentleman, and the small, subtle ways he looked out for her made up for his lack of passenger skills.

"Back to your hotel or are you coming home with me?" she asked when she'd started the car.

"I'll come home with you. That baklava looked good, so I think you owe me some dessert."

"Try not to leave fingernail marks in my door panel on the way home," she teased, pulling out into traffic.

Three hours later, a very naked Will cupped her breast and held her close to him. "Are the fingernail marks in my back payback for your door?"

She hadn't quite recovered enough from her third

orgasm of the night to come up with a witty response, so she chuckled and made a sound that was probably an agreement.

"Better than baklava," he murmured against her hair.

She was sleepy, her muscles languid from sex and the heat of his body, so she might have nodded off until Will kissed the back of her neck. It was always the last thing he did before he got up and summoned an Uber, getting dressed while he waited.

Grabbing his wrist, she stopped him from rolling away from her. "Don't go."

His body tensed against hers for a few seconds, and then his arm relaxed as he kissed her neck again. "Are you sure?"

Was she sure it was a good idea? No. She'd never had a man spend the night in this apartment because it was a relationship line she'd never wanted to cross before. But was she sure she didn't want him to leave? Absolutely. "My alarm goes off early, but I'll make you breakfast."

He settled against her, his breath tickling her hair. "Or I'll make you breakfast while you get ready for work."

This man's a keeper was the last coherent thought she had before she fell asleep.

8

A few days later, Kristen let herself into her father's house, or—as she thought of it, sometimes with humor but quite often not—the Erik Burke Shrine. She was fairly certain if she looked hard enough, she might find a picture of her somewhere, but she'd bet good money it would be a picture taken with Erik before or after a big hockey game.

Most of the time, she was okay with it. She'd long ago come to terms with the fact Lamont Burke was living vicariously through his son's success—that being Erik Burke's dad was the most important aspect of his identity—but accidentally having the best sex of her life with a hockey player already had her on edge.

She'd also had a pretty brutal workday she might resent less if she had the title and the pay that went with the amount and kind of work she did. Being summoned to the shrine by a terse text message hadn't done much to improve her mood.

Of course her father was in what she called "the situation room," which was furnished with two recliners, a table between them, and three televisions. A dry-erase board with a diagram of the ice permanently printed on it hung on the wall, and that was it. This room was for watching game tapes and strategizing.

"Kristen!" He looked surprised when he finally looked up from the legal pad he was reading. She knew from experience it was a list of all the mistakes he perceived Erik had made during the last game so they could review them.

"You demanded I stop by," she reminded him. "I'm here."

"I wanted to talk to you," he said, tossing the legal pad on the side table as he pushed himself out of the chair.

She turned and walked back to the kitchen, knowing he'd follow rather than invite her to sit in the other recliner. She'd never crossed the threshold of the situation room, and she saw no reason to start now. After grabbing a bottle of water from the fridge, she leaned against the counter and looked at him expectantly.

"We're getting ready to leave for St. Louis," he said.

"Did you really have me come all the way here after work so you could tell me that? I know you're getting ready for the All-Star weekend because I talked to Erik a few hours ago." She talked to her brother almost every day, a fact her father never seemed to consider.

"I want to know where the situation with you and Cross Lecroix stands before I leave town."

"It still stands in the *my personal business, so don't worry about it* column."

Temper flared in his eyes, and it might have intimidated a lot of people into submission, but Kristen had given up on pleasing Lamont Burke a very long time ago. She put up with him because he was her father and because totally cutting him out of her life would make things harder for

Eric, but she wasn't emotionally invested in his opinion of her anymore.

"It's going to be a big weekend for your brother, and he'll be in the spotlight. I don't want you two back here trying to distract attention from him."

She snorted and rolled her eyes. "Are we doing that again? I'm not jealous of the attention Erik gets, and I'm not trying to sabotage his game."

"You don't think bringing Cross Lecroix into our lives sabotages his game?"

"He's in *my* life, not *ours*. And no, it's not sabotaging Erik." She held up her hand before he could speak again. "And if you think I would do or say anything to hurt Erik, you don't know me at all. If you keep barking up that tree, I will walk out of here, and it will be the last time you ever see me. And *you* can explain why to Erik."

"You've always been difficult."

"Thanks for noticing." When he just stared at her, silently fuming, she smiled. "So, is that it? I have plans with Cross tonight."

She used the name just to annoy her dad, and it worked. His skin flushed, and she watched him struggle to hold back the angry words she knew he wanted to fling at her. But she wasn't joking about walking out, and he knew it. And he also knew that Erik wouldn't stand for it.

"Dad. Come on," she said in a much softer tone because suddenly she was really tired of all this and wanted to go home. "I love Erik. And if I thought for a second Will's interest in me came from him wanting to piss Erik off, I'd dump his ass in a heartbeat. None of us wanted that story to come out, and all three of us are doing our best to *not* be a story again. Go enjoy your weekend in St. Louis and don't worry about this."

"I guess I'll have to trust your judgment on this one," he muttered, also backing down. "Are you going to watch the events? At least the game?"

"I never do, Dad." She glanced at her watch and then put the cap back on her water so she could take it with her. "I really do have to go, though. Have fun."

Her building was far enough away from her dad's house so she could use a little speed and a lot of loud music to take the edge off the post-Lamont mood, but she was still a little edgy when she got home. And she only had about forty minutes left before Will showed up to take her out to dinner.

After pinning up her hair and taking one of the fastest showers ever, she put on a pair of black leggings and a blue tunic top the same color as her eyes. How Will was dressed would determine which accessories she paired with it. If he showed up in jeans, she'd throw on comfy boots and a coat. If he dressed up, some dress boots, jewelry and a scarf would fancy her up enough to match.

Will was a few minutes early, and she was glad she hadn't put on a little black dress, because he was not only in jeans but wearing a Baltimore Harriers hoodie. She didn't say anything about it, but it struck her as odd because he preferred to blend in and not draw attention to who he was, especially in a city that hated him.

He paused to kiss her on his way through the door, and she noticed how tired he looked. Not just physically tired, either, but a weariness that showed in his eyes. It could be his shoulder, she thought as he hung up his coat and set his boots on the mat.

"You smell delicious," he said, pulling out a kitchen chair to sit in.

"I took a quick shower to wash the workday off. How did your day go? You look beat tonight."

He gave a little shrug that did nothing to dispel the impression he was exhausted. "One of those days, I guess. Sometimes it's incredibly rewarding but really hard at the same time."

"Did you get in a fight today? Maybe punch a guy in the face and knock him out?"

He gave her a long look she couldn't quite decipher. "Something like that. You know how hockey is. Just a bunch of guys slamming each other into the boards."

It was *hurt* she heard in his voice. Not pain from his shoulder or offense at her dismissal of his sport. There was more to it than that.

She sat sideways on his lap and draped her arm around his shoulders. "Tell me what actually happened today."

"I thought you already made up your mind about that."

"I was being a bitch because I had to go see my dad today, which always makes me feel shitty about hockey all over again, and I'm sorry." She ran her fingers up into his hair and scratched his scalp with her fingernails. "Tell me what happened today. Is it your shoulder?"

"No." He closed his eyes for a moment, breathing deeply. "I went to the children's hospital to visit a little girl."

She stopped scratching, dropping her hand to rub the back of his neck. "What is she there for?"

"Leukemia. Her family moved here two years ago from Baltimore, and she's still a diehard Harriers fan. When the hospital found out I was in town, they contacted the Skimmers' office."

"She must have been beside herself when you walked in."

He picked up his cell phone and pulled up a photo of

him with his arm around a little girl sitting on a hospital bed. She was pale and a Harriers knit cap covered her head, but her smile practically lit up the picture. And that explained why he was wearing a Harriers hoodie around Boston.

"She looks like she's having one of the happiest moments of her life." She tilted her head so she could see his face. "Thanks to you."

"I don't even do anything." His jaw clenched and then relaxed as she stroked his neck. "I love visiting the kids. Their lives are so hard right now, and if I can cheer them up, I'm in. It's awesome to see them smile. But it's also...tough."

"It must be nice for their parents to see them light up like that, too."

"Yeah. She's a fierce girl, this one. One hell of a fighter." His gaze was on the phone screen, and she knew he'd be keeping tabs on the kid.

"My brother doesn't do very many hospital visits."

"Not everybody does. Or can. The machines and tubes and shit freak some guys out, and some people just aren't comfortable around children. Kids are super intuitive, and they know when you're forcing it."

"It was hard for Erik when my mom was sick, too. She was sick for a long time."

He pulled her against his chest, wrapping his arms around her. "His foundation raises a lot of money and awareness for pediatric cancer support, though."

She smiled. "Did you just defend my brother?"

"I'll use double the mouthwash later."

They laughed together, and since she was pressed against his body, she could feel him relaxing. She wanted him to *keep* relaxing. "How do you feel about pizza deliveries and movies?"

He made a sound similar to a sound he made during sex. "I approve of both in a general sense, but I'm very much in favor of them right now."

"What are the chances we agree on toppings?" She pulled back so she could see his face, which already looked a little more relaxed.

"I'm pretty boring, I guess. A classic pepperoni and cheese is my favorite."

"Sex *and* pizza compatibility," she said, getting up off his lap so she could get her phone and place the order. "Next up, seeing if our movie compatibility is as strong as we think it is."

Two hours later, there was an empty pizza box on the coffee table, the apartment smelled like fresh popcorn, and they were both in a far better mood. Will had that effect on her, she thought. She enjoyed having him around, and not just in the bedroom.

As she watched a limo racing to escape a crumbling fictional city on the screen, she felt a pang of anxiety that had nothing to do with the characters in the limo.

Kristen couldn't quite put her finger on the exact moment her relationship with Will had changed, but she couldn't deny that somewhere along the way, it had.

They were fake dating behind closed doors now. They were acting like a couple when nobody was watching—when it wasn't necessary to keep up the pretense. They'd been together every night since the first night, going out for dinner in a variety of places before going back to her place, where they'd fall into bed. He'd leave early in the morning so they could both get ready for the day's work, and then they'd do it all again.

Now here they were, cuddled up on her couch with a movie on. His arm was draped on the back of the couch, and his hand was resting on her shoulder. A bowl of popcorn was balanced on his thigh and when they reached for some at the same time and their hands touched, it wasn't even awkward.

They were dating. *Actually* dating. And she had no idea how or when it had happened.

But there was no reason for them to be together right now, laughing at how awful the disaster movie was that they'd chosen to watch. No reason for her to be sitting against his body instead of at the other end of the couch.

No reason at all, except that she looked forward to spending time with him. She liked it. She liked *him*.

Shit.

That wasn't part of the deal. Making her life look "respectable" for her superconservative boss was the objective. Great sex and numerous orgasms were a sweet bonus. She enjoyed the hell out of his company in bed and had seen no reason to deprive herself of him as long as he was in town. She just hadn't expected to enjoy his company *out* of bed.

"Everything okay?" he asked, turning the TV's volume down.

"Yeah. Why?"

"Well, you got tense all of a sudden. And you just randomly said 'shit,' which is usually a dead giveaway something's wrong."

She hadn't realized she'd said it out loud, and her brain flailed for a lie—anything but the truth because she wasn't ready for that kind of confession. "Sorry. I just remembered a thing I need to do at work."

The answer must have satisfied him because he turned the volume back up.

Kristen concentrated on relaxing since he could feel the

tension in her body, but it wasn't easy because she couldn't stop thinking about her realization that she liked dating him. Or fake dating him. Pretending to fake date. She didn't even know anymore.

"THAT WAS A GREAT MOVIE," Will said when the end credits started rolling.

"You're being sarcastic, right?"

"No. You didn't like it?" Judging by her expression, she not only didn't like it, but was judging him pretty harshly. "You have to admit, it was entertaining."

"The wrong kind of entertaining, though."

He shrugged. "I don't know if there are wrong kinds of entertainment. If I was entertained, it's all good."

"I spent most of the second half thinking about the ice cream I have in the freezer, but I was too comfortable to get up and get it."

He groaned. "I ate too much pizza, but now that you've said the words *ice cream*, I could go for some maple walnut right now."

"Ew." Her expression made it clear she wasn't a fan. "No, I have mint chocolate chip, and you have terrible taste in ice cream. Is it because you're Canadian?"

He laughed. "They have maple walnut ice cream in the US, you know."

"But it's probably Canada's fault. Don't even get me started on your potato chip flavors."

"You're quite the food snob for a woman who eats frozen Brussel sprouts." He grunted when she elbowed him in the ribs. "And speaking of Canada, don't be surprised if you come home one day to find two Canadian women who look kind of like me camped out in your building lobby, waiting for you."

"I think I *would* be surprised, even with a heads-up. Should I run and hide?"

He laughed. "From my mother and sister? No."

"Okay, but why will they be camped out, waiting for me?"

"Because my mother is beside herself that I'm dating a woman she's never met, and when you throw in the fact you're a Burke, she's losing a little sleep over it. And if she loses sleep, everybody in the family loses sleep. And Cassie would come with her instead of my dad because they think he's too much of a pushover." He frowned. "But nobody's coming out of it with a bruised jaw, if that's what you're asking."

"Wouldn't it be easier if you just told your family the truth? I'm not really comfortable with you lying to your mom. I mean, none of your family, really. But especially your mother."

"I love my mom, but if ever there was a woman who can't keep a secret, it's Paulette Lecroix. Between Facebook and how excited she gets when somebody asks her about me, we'd end up in an even bigger scandal than we started with."

"How often does anybody try to interview her anymore, though?"

"Ouch." That hurt a little.

"I didn't mean that the way it sounded. It's just that the media's been telling your story for years, and they might think she doesn't have anything new to add?"

"Except for how my family feels about me dating the sister of my biggest professional rival—the guy I've been swapping punches and hard checks with for years. Hockey might not register on the tabloid media's radar, but this is the kind of story that can get sports sites some clicks, you know?"

"It's ridiculous."

"It's ridiculous and it's part of the job, but at least it doesn't physically hurt." He was trying to be funny, but she didn't laugh.

"Why did you choose to play hockey? And it's a genuine question, not a snarky one."

"Because I'm good at it." He tried to come up with something profound, but it was just that simple. "That's it. I'm good at it, I love it, and they pay me to do it. It also paid for college."

She shrugged. "My brother didn't go to college."

"Trust me, I know."

"I was just making conversation. Not everything's a competition."

"With Erik, it is. And just so you know, he didn't go straight into the league because he was better than me. He's never been *better* than me. But he was raised to be a hockey player. I was raised to get a hockey scholarship."

"Is there a difference?"

"On the ice? No. But when it comes to making choices, I think there is."

She tilted her head to look at him, looking genuinely interested. "In what way?"

"When they realized I not only loved hockey but was good enough to play in college, they sacrificed so much for the chance I'd get a degree because nobody in my family ever had one. My dad took every chance at overtime. My mom would work second jobs here and there, part-time. It's incredibly expensive to raise a hockey player, especially on what they made. The gear. Fees. Just the gas to drive my ass around. When I got my college scholarship, they were not only proud but so relieved. They'd accomplished their goal, which wasn't about the game at all. Even though I don't use the degree to do more than keep an eye on my business manager, I owed my parents that framed certificate on the wall because *they* earned it."

"What about your sister? Did you owe her, too?"

There was some bite in her tone, and he twisted his body a little so he could see her face and the tension in her jaw and cheekbones. "What do you mean?"

"What sacrifices did *she* have to make so you could get that certificate on the wall?"

He was about to make a joke about getting to have a professional hockey player for a big brother, but his brain kicked into high gear just in time to stop the words from coming out of his mouth. Having a professional hockey player for a big brother might be a big part of why Kristen hated hockey, and there was a good chance being flippant about it was going to put him on the wrong side of her front door with his clothes in his arms.

"It wasn't easy on her, I'm sure. She was in chorus and was a cheerleader for the basketball team, so winter was busy. My parents had to trade off a lot so one of them was at each event, meaning she rarely had both parents there. Neither did I, but we made it work. Sometimes our neighbor had to drive Cassie around if I had a tournament out of town, but we all helped her with her lawn and keeping her house up and stuff."

"I guess having two parents helped."

Will closed his eyes, belatedly remembering a profile of Erik Burke that mentioned his mom had passed away when he was a kid. Now he wished he'd paid more attention to the stories about Burke's background, since he shared that childhood with Kristen.

"I did a few extracurricular activities when I was in school, but my dad rarely showed up," she said. "And nothing that cost a lot of money, since there wasn't any left over after Erik's hockey expenses."

He wanted stroke her hair, but he suspected if he interrupted her or tried to give her sympathy, she'd shut down, and he wanted to hear it. He wanted to understand a little more about why she hated the sport that was his entire life.

"We moved to a new place right before I started middle school," she continued. "My dad wanted Erik in a high school with a top hockey team, so we just...moved. Dad took a pay cut and the cost of living was a lot higher, so I had no friends, no money and didn't feel safe in the sketchy apartment building we lived in. I spent a lot of time alone with the doors locked and a lot of time doing my brother's homework so he could be on the ice."

"That sounds lonely. I can see why you'd have some resentment toward the sport."

"That's putting it mildly. I guess it worked out. Erik's living his dream—or Dad's dream, since the line's a bit fuzzy there—and I have this apartment."

Will wasn't brave enough to ask her outright if Erik had bought it for her, but it sure sounded that way.

She chuckled softly. "Probably thanks to Dad, Erik's not great with expressing emotion, so he wrote me a letter. An actual paper letter sent through the mail, with a few pictures of the place. He said he knew I'd spent a lot of time alone in a shithole growing up and that he'd been putting money aside for six years until he found a beautiful place he thought I'd like and that would make me feel safe and that nobody could take away from me. And he hadn't signed the papers because he wanted it to be my choice and to only have my name on it, and he said if I wanted it, to let him know."

He wasn't surprised her voice choked off, since he was feeling a bit emotional himself. About Erik freakin' Burke, of all people. "Damn."

"Of course my first reaction was to refuse to let him throw his hockey money at me," she said with a laugh. "But then I realized it wasn't some kind of grandiose gesture to show off or even an apology for shit that was mostly our dad's fault. It was his way of saying thank you, so I accepted it."

"It's a very nice thank you," he said. "And since you gave him a key, now you're stuck with me for a while to keep everybody's name out of the mud."

She laughed, as he'd hoped she would. "Let's not get things twisted here. You know as well as I do the only name that would be dragged through the mud is mine. And I'm not stuck with you. I'm choosing to go along with this charade because I'm not done with you yet and this is the best way to get what I want."

"Which is me."

She jabbed her elbow into his side. "Which is orgasms not of the do-it-yourself variety and you happen to be particularly good at providing them."

"I should have *better than a vibrator* added to my press kit."

"Probably see a nice bump in jersey sales." She laughed. "You could even expand your branded merchandise."

"I don't see the league letting me brand that kind of merch, but I bet I could secretly have a limited edition, custom Cross Lecroix vibrator made for you."

She ran her hand up his thigh, managing to skim her

fingernails over his balls before stroking the length of his dick. The denim between his flesh and her palm wasn't enough to keep him from being instantly hard.

He was pretty sure a time when he wouldn't desperately want her didn't exist.

"I'll stick with the real thing," she said in a husky voice.

"I get the feeling I'm about to be sent to bed with no ice cream."

"You must have been naughty." She stood and took his hand to haul him to his feet.

"We could take the ice cream to bed *with* us," he managed to say with a straight face.

She laughed. "By the time I'm done with you, neither of us will have the strength left to change the sheets. Think long and hard about whether you want to sleep in a puddle of mint chocolate chip."

"We'll have it for breakfast," he decided, and then he picked her up and carried her toward the bedroom.

He was halfway there when he realized there had been only the slightest twinge of protest from his shoulder. It was good news, because proving he was pain-free and had full range of motion was the key to getting back to his team.

But as he dropped Kristen on the bed and then covered her body with his so he looked into her sparkling blue eyes, there was a part of him that didn't want to celebrate his time in Boston coming to an end soon.

9

Kristen knew what tonight it was. Even without the text messages blowing up Will's phone and causing him to get increasingly quiet over the course of the day, she would have known it was time for the All-Star Game. It was pretty much a Burke high holiday, though she usually opted out.

She'd talked to Erik on the phone that morning, while Will was in the shower. She'd called her brother to wish him luck, just as she always did before a game that meant something to him, but Will had yet to mention any of the All-Star events, even in passing. He certainly hadn't brought up the fact Erik had won the accuracy competition in the skills events last night. But she assumed the constant attention to his phone meant he was either getting notifications or he had teammates in St. Louis who were sending him updates.

He hadn't mentioned watching it, though she would have broken her *no hockey on my TV* rule if he brought it up. She wasn't going to volunteer to sit through it if she didn't have to, though.

"Do you want to get out of here?"

He looked up from his phone when she spoke, his brow furrowed. His expression cleared within seconds, but it confirmed her suspicion his mood was tied to whatever was on his screen. "Where do you want to go?"

Unfortunately, she hadn't thought that far ahead. "I don't know. We could see a movie or a show. There are museums and the aquarium and... Hell, I don't know."

"I'm not being very good company," he said, leaning forward to toss the phone onto the coffee table.

"You don't have to be, you know," she told Will, sitting next to him on the couch sideways so she could see him, with her legs tucked under her. "I know you'd rather be in St. Louis right now."

He leaned back against the couch with a heavy sigh. "It's not easy not being there, I guess."

"Are all the messages you're getting from there?"

"Yeah. Mitchell's there, along with a few other guys I know. Dev Mitchell, he's been with the Harriers almost as long as I have. We're pretty close friends."

"I recognize the name."

He chuckled. "I don't imagine your brother's a big fan of his, either."

"I don't know if Erik's talked about him a lot. Some, I'm sure. But I also hear things. Sports recaps if I have the news on. Televisions in bars. I just know I've heard the name before. Did he get your spot?"

"That's not exactly how it works, but let's just say if I was healthy, he'd probably be sitting on the couch with his wife, getting text messages from me." As he said it, his phone vibrated, and she saw his body tense as if he was going to reach for it, but he didn't. "I should probably just turn that off."

"Do you want to watch it?"

"Were you planning to?"

"No," she said honestly, and then she shrugged. "But we can. I'll make popcorn."

He frowned. "Popcorn?"

"Fine, I can order some wings, and we can drink beer and get buffalo sauce on my couch."

"That's how you watch hockey." He rested his arm on the back of the couch and reached for her hair, twirling it around his finger. "But we don't have to watch the game. That's not exactly your idea of a fun Saturday night."

"Not everything's about me." She laughed when he gave her a very exaggerated look of shock. "Be honest with me. Do you *want* to watch the game, or will it just make you feel shitty because you're missing it?"

"I'd like to watch it. I know all the guys playing, and I don't usually get to enjoy it from the comfort of a couch because, let's be honest—" He paused to raise his eyebrow in a way that would have come off as arrogant if it wasn't ruined by the fact he was trying to keep a straight face. "I'm usually in it."

She groaned and got to her feet. "Okay, let's make a deal. You walk down to the market with me because we're almost out of food and you drank the last of my milk. When we get back, we'll order in pizza and wings and watch the game."

His expression brightened, and his dark eyes crinkled when he smiled. "That sounds like a hell of a good deal."

Before she could walk away, intending to make a list of things to tide them over until she made a proper run to the grocery store, he snagged her hand and pulled her onto his lap.

She braced her hands on the back of the couch, one arm on either side of his head, as his hands skimmed over her back and then cupped her ass. "You're going to make me forget what I need to put on the shopping list."

"Milk," he said. "And some other stuff."

He kissed her before she could point out it was the other stuff she needed to figure out, but as soon as his lips touched hers, she stopped caring. That's what delivery was for.

She moaned when he caught her lip between his teeth with just enough pressure to make her squirm before kissing that spot. His tongue slipped between her lips, and she buried her hand in his hair, her fingers sliding through the soft strands.

But when he slid his hand up the back of her shirt, stroking bare skin, she ignored the hunger that was always there but definitely flared up when he had his hands on her, and she broke off the kiss.

"You're trying to get out of going to the market," she said.

"No, I'm not. I'm just...delaying our departure a little."

Laughing, she slapped at the hand he was not-very-stealthily sliding up to her breast. "I'm not getting naked and then getting dressed again to go to the store."

"Milk is overrated anyway."

"You won't be saying that when you have to drink your coffee black in the morning."

She watched his expression as the battle waged—the erection currently pressed against the inside of her thigh versus waking up to no milk for their coffee—and then he sighed. "I hate coffee with no milk."

"Then do some algebra in your head or something while I make a list." She climbed off his lap and moved out of his reach before he could change his mind.

"I was always really good at algebra, you know. It's way too easy for it to distract me from picturing you naked."

When she gave him a skeptical look, he shrugged. "What? Didn't I mention I got my degree with high honors?"

"Then think about something hard." Before he could even open his mouth, she rolled her eyes and turned away. "Save it."

His laughter filled the apartment and she shook her head, opening the shopping list app on her phone and adding milk before opening the fridge to figure out what else they needed. But when she went to open the pantry, the box she'd set on the end of the counter caught her eye. It was a gift from Annie and Kara, one of Kristen's other friends, and she'd forgotten about it until now.

She'd have to remember that gift when they got back from the market, she thought, because what was in that box would definitely cheer him up.

"FOR A WOMAN WHO HATES HOCKEY, you sure have a lot to say about it." Will couldn't remember the last time he'd enjoyed an All-Star Game he wasn't skating in. It had been years, though. Before his attendance had become something of a given and watching had reinforced his drive to make the cut.

But watching a game with Kristen was a hell of a lot more fun than he would have thought. While she might have chosen to turn her back on the sport, it was very obvious she'd been raised a Burke.

"What's the point of bringing all the best players in the league—except you, of course—in to play if you're going to bring refs that don't know what freakin' tripping looks like?"

He tried not to laugh, but he couldn't help it. "You do know this game doesn't really count, right? It's just for fun."

"I'm sure the guy that just kissed the ice thought it was *super* fun."

"Burke got a goal. That should put you in a good mood. And Mitchell got one."

She sighed as the network cut to a commercial, and she stood up. Usually she was curled against him when they watched TV, but she had a tendency to use her hands a lot when she was ranting, and the last thing he needed was the *Hometown Hoser* finding out he'd taken another shot—even accidentally—to the face from another Burke.

When she started gathering up the debris from the pizza and wings they'd been snacking on for an hour, he was going to get up, but she waved him back. "I've got this. I can work off some of my frustration with this stupid sport."

He wasn't about to miss that opening. "You know what's a good way to work off frustration?"

"So smooth, Lecroix," she said, rolling her eyes for good measure. "However can I resist such a charming line?"

"Can't blame a guy for trying."

"Watch your game. I'm going to load the dishwasher and then change into TV-watching clothes. I ate too much."

When she was done in the kitchen and went into the bedroom, he thought about following her, but the announcer started talking about the season Mitchell was having, and Will turned his attention back to the television. He was happy as hell for his friend, but the need to be back with his team was a constant, nagging ache that never quite went away.

Movement in the corner of his eye caught his attention, and he realized Kristen was back. He was about to make a smart-ass comment about how much he'd missed her commentary, but when he turned to look at her, his brain stopped giving him any signals except instant lust.

The Harriers red and white home jersey hung halfway down her thighs, but when she lifted her arms to show off the emblem in the center, the hem lifted almost enough so he could see if she was wearing panties under it.

It didn't matter if she was because she wouldn't be for long.

"My friends couldn't believe I didn't have my boyfriend's jersey, so they ordered me one," she said, the corners of her mouth turning up as he pushed himself to his feet.

Boyfriend. It didn't matter that it had started as a lie they told the rest of the world. That's exactly who he was. And his girl was wearing his jersey.

"Do you like it?" she asked, and just as he was about to reach her, she turned around so he could see the back.

LECROIX.

Seeing his name in big block letters across her back triggered something deep inside of him—something raw and primal—and he gathered the fabric below his number in his fist and pulled her backward until her body hit his.

When her ass ground against his erection through the fly of his jeans—and no, she wasn't wearing anything under the jersey—they both moaned, and he gathered her hair in his fist, lifting it off the letters.

"I guess you *do* like it," she said in that low, husky voice that forced him to undo his jeans just to relieve some of the pressure. "Do you get off on me wearing your number?"

He got off on her wearing his *name*, but he wasn't sure he was ready to talk about how hard that realization hit him. And he wasn't sure how she'd feel about that. "I get off on *you*. Everything about you turns me on. Your laugh. The way you give your hair a little twist when you pull it free of your collar. And yes, I get off on seeing you in my jersey."

"I don't want to distract you from your game," she said in a far-too-innocent voice, considering she'd taken his free hand and was guiding it under the hem of the jersey, eliminating any doubt she wasn't wearing underwear.

He tightened his other hand in her hair and tilted her head to the side so he could kiss her neck. "What game?"

When he dipped his hand between her thighs and she made a low groaning sound in her throat, he was surprised his knees didn't buckle. She was wet already, and he stroked her until she whimpered and tried to pull away.

"You started it," he whispered against her ear. "I think *you* get off on wearing my jersey, too."

"The way you looked at me..." The words trailed off into a moan as he pressed his fingertips over her clit.

Then he withdrew his hand and turned her around to face the couch before pressing down on her back to bend her over. She braced her hands on the arm of the couch, and he ran his hands down the back of the jersey, allowing himself a few seconds to savor that rush of possessiveness, before he got down on his knees behind her.

He heard her gasp when he closed his mouth over her pussy, and he sucked hard on her clit before circling his tongue around it. Alternating between licking and sucking, he didn't let up until her skin was hot under his touch and her legs were trembling.

Then he brought his hand into it, pressing his thumb deep into her until she said his name in a pleading tone that almost sent him over the edge. He withdrew his thumb so he could circle her clit with it, his tongue dipping inside of her until he felt her muscles trembling and she made that sound that always rocked his world.

He curled his free arm around her thighs, holding her while his thumb circled her clit so she wouldn't fall while the orgasm racked her body. And when it had passed, he ran his hand over the cheek of her ass and gave her a moment to catch her breath.

"Jesus, Will," she muttered against the battered leather before pushing herself upright.

When she turned in his arms, her flushed face turning up to face him, Will's dick throbbed so badly, he was afraid he was going to embarrass himself. "I don't have a condom, so let's take this to the bedroom."

She frowned and pulled him to the front of the couch. "We're supposed to be watching the game."

Will had forgotten there even *was* a game the second he'd laid eyes on her, and he hoped this wasn't some kind of twisted revenge plot she'd come up with to punish him for having hockey on her television. Sitting through a game in his current condition could be harmful to his health.

But then she yanked his open jeans down, taking his boxer briefs with them, and gave him a little shove. Since his pants were around his knees, he didn't have a lot of choice but to fall onto the couch cushion.

It only took her a few seconds to pull the clothes off of his legs and toss them aside. Then she bent over and ran her hands up his thighs. His knees spread wider without any conscious thought on his part, and she settled between them.

"Now you can watch the game," she teased.

Yet he wasn't watching anything but Kristen as she wrapped her hand around his dick and stroked the length with a firm grip. Her tongue flicked over her bottom lip, and he stared at her mouth as she lowered it so excruciatingly slowly that he felt himself straining upward to meet her.

He closed his eyes as her lips surrounded him, and as she took in his length, he knew there wasn't an algebraic equation ever written that could distract him from the wet heat of her mouth. Savoring the moment and making it last was out of the question.

Opening his eyes, he pushed her hair back from her face so he could watch as her mouth moved up and down his shaft, her tongue flicking over the tip in between each stroke. He whispered her name and then groaned when she wrapped her hand around the base of his dick, squeezing as her lips slid down to meet her fingers over and over, each time a little faster.

His hips bucked when he came, and she held him with one hand against his thigh as she swallowed, stroking him softly until the tremors passed and he let his head fall against the cushion.

When she stood, he shifted to his side and hauled her down to cuddle against him. It was slightly awkward, since he was wearing a shirt and no pants, but he just wanted to hold her for a few minutes.

But then she made a satisfied sound and ran her hand down the arm he'd flung across her before lacing their fingers together, and suddenly he didn't care that he wasn't wearing pants.

He was going to hold Kristen for as long as she'd let him.

10

"I swear this place gets louder every time we come here." Annie frowned in the direction of the three women screeching with laughter. "Or I'm getting old and cranky. Am I old and cranky, Kristen?"

"We're the same age, and we are absolutely not getting old. But you've always been cranky."

"True."

They'd been coming to this very trendy and upscale bar once every two or three months because it gave them a chance to really dress up. And also because the dirty martinis were fabulous and the patrons were slightly less handsy than at other places they visited. And Kristen had never invited Annie to Firewall with her because, even though she was a good friend, they worked together, and it was Kristen's work-free happy place.

And now it would always be the place she'd met Will, she realized when thinking of Firewall automatically triggered an image of him in his gray Henley, head bent over his phone to read about Abigail Adams.

She should have gone to his game.

He hadn't outright asked her. And he hadn't pushed back when he brought it up and she changed the subject. But wouldn't that be the only reason he brought it up at all? It wasn't as if they spent their time together sitting around and talking hockey.

And Annie would have understood if she'd rescheduled this girls' night out. Hell, she probably would have been thrilled since she was always telling Kristen she should get out there and date. *Really* date, and not just scratch the itch occasionally.

But sitting at a Skimmers game, knowing the camera would eventually find her and her face would be on the Jumbotron, wasn't high on the list of things she wanted to do. Once the crowd knew she was there, there would be whispers and people in the rows in front of her taking weird-angle selfies as if she wouldn't notice they were really trying to sneak a picture of Erik Burke's sister cheering on Cross Lecroix.

No thank you.

But it was a big deal to him, coming back after an injury the way he was. And without his team, in a hostile city. She should have been the friendly face in the crowd for him.

A dirty martini later, Will was still on her mind. She couldn't shake the feeling in the pit of her stomach that she was doing the wrong thing right now.

"What's the matter with you tonight? You're so tense, I'm afraid somebody's going to bump into you and you're just going to break into pieces."

"Nothing. Just...work and stuff."

"I work *with* you, so I know all about that, and I also know it doesn't make you like this. Stressed and pissed off? Yes. But you're wound extra tight tonight. Is it the hockey player everybody's been talking about?"

"Yes and no, I guess."

"Yeah, I'm going to need one more drink and a *lot* more detail."

Kristen had no problem with another round of cocktails, but the details were going to be a problem. Annie was the closest thing she'd ever had to a best friend, even though they'd only known each other for a couple of years, but the truth of her relationship with Will was such a secret, he couldn't even tell his parents. It wouldn't be right for her to confide in Annie, no matter how much she wanted to.

But she could tell part of it.

"I didn't know he was a hockey player when we met," she said. "You know how I feel about hockey."

"Oh, that kind of sucks. What did he tell you he did?"

"He didn't lie or anything. I told him I didn't care what he did, if you know what I mean. The relationship wasn't supposed to go that deep."

"Obviously it went a little bit deep, since you not only know what he does, but you're dating now."

"A little bit deep," she muttered. "I guess you could say that."

"So, are you breaking up with him?"

Eventually. That was the plan, though it was weird how she was already having trouble picturing herself day-to-day without him. He hadn't been in her life very long, but he seemed to fill it up somehow, and she knew it was going to feel very empty when he left.

"No, I just...the hockey's a problem for me." After taking a sip of the fresh cocktail the server set in front of her, Kristen met Annie's gaze. "He's playing tonight. Right now. He mentioned it because it's his first game since his injury, and I was afraid he was going to ask me outright to go, so I changed the subject."

"Ouch." Annie winced. "You know I'm totally Team Kristen, but that had to get under his skin a bit. It would probably mean a lot to have his girlfriend cheering him on at his game, you know?"

There was no way to push back against the girlfriend designation without telling more than she should, so Kristen shrugged. "He knows about my family. He knows how I feel about the game."

"Maybe he thought you'd care more about him than you do about not liking hockey."

Ouch. That hurt a little. "Have I ever told you martinis make you mean?"

"No, but I've been told they make me honest," Annie said, winking at Kristen over the rim of her martini glass.

"I shouldn't be here," Kristen admitted. "I should have gone to the stupid game."

"If we leave right now, can you still make it? Do the ride-share apps let you pick the fastest driver?"

"No, they don't. But if you're okay with it, I'm going to go. Even if I miss the end of the game, I'll get there before he leaves the locker room. I can at least be there when it's over."

"Call for a car, and I'll get the bill," Annie said. "You can totally make it."

Once she was in the backseat of an Uber, she realized how ridiculous she was going to look walking into a hockey arena. Little black dress. Black heels. A long black coat that wasn't really warm enough for the weather but looked good on her. She would definitely stand out in the crowd.

She'd just dodge the camera people and hope her face didn't show up on the big screen.

~

WILL WAS the last guy left in the locker room, and he soaked in the blessed silence. He liked being alone after the chaos and noise of a game, to the point it was not only something of a post-game ritual, but also pretty widely known, so the other guys didn't linger. Between being called back out on the ice so often to be honored as a highlight player and then the press questions, by the time Will went in the locker room, a lot of others were already on their way out.

He sat on the bench, working up the energy to take a shower. The aches and pains were already making themselves known, though he was gratified they were just the normal twinges and sore spots that came with the sport. His shoulder seemed solid, and as long as he kept following the instructions he'd been given for taking a little extra care with it, he felt pretty confident it wouldn't be an issue in the future.

Of course, one of the instructions was to stop dropping gloves with Erik Burke, and he wasn't sure how that one was going to go. Especially the first time they met on the ice after he returned to Baltimore and Kristen wasn't between them to calm them down.

The locker room door swung open, but he didn't bother looking up. Probably one of the guys forgot something in a locker, or it was somebody from the equipment crew. But the sharp staccato sound of high heels on a tile floor got his attention, and he looked up to see Kristen walking toward him in a sleeveless black dress that hugged her curves so sweetly, his mouth watered. A long black coat was slung over her arm, and he really hoped she'd been wearing that wherever she was before here.

"Hey," she said, walking so close to him, she ended up straddling one leg, a heel on either side of the skate he hadn't bothered taking off yet.

He put his hands on her legs, getting turned on again by the way his fingertips made dents in her thighs, before he looked up at her face. Well, at how fantastic her breasts looked in the deep V-neck dress and *then* at her face. "How did you get in here?"

"I'm Erik Burke's sister. Usually it's a giant pain in the ass, but it has perks in the hockey world." She shrugged. "I was just hanging around, waiting for you to come out, but the last guy that came out recognized me and said you were alone in here and that nobody would bother us. He winked, so there's a good chance within ten minutes, everybody involved with the Skimmers who has a phone will think we're having sex in the locker room."

He chuckled. "It all adds to the legend."

"Yeah, well we can stay in here for whatever amount of time protects the great Cross Lecroix legacy, but we're not *actually* having sex in here. My vagina wants nothing to do with being exposed in a hockey locker room."

"Good call, though it's still a shame. You look amazing." He twisted his torso, hoping his back wouldn't stiffen too much. "Do me a favor, though, and keep your expectations for tonight low. The guys seem to get younger and faster every year, and I'm beat."

"Pretty sure I saw you knock one of those young kids on his ass."

He grinned. "There's something to be said for experience."

"How did your shoulder hold up?"

"It's good." It was ready for a strong stream of very hot water, but it was good. He rolled his head slowly, to stretch his neck, and his gaze caught on the way her feet looked so small and sexy compared to his big skates. "So, can you skate? You've never said if you learned to skate when your brother did."

"Of course I can skate. Who do you think was between the pipes while my dad was teaching Erik to take a hit?" She laughed as she glanced down at herself. "But I'm not going to prove it tonight, since I'm not exactly dressed for skating."

He reached out with one hand, wanting to feel her hair wrapped around his fingers. "Another time."

"Even if you pull my hair, there's no locker room banging. I ninety percent mean that." He tugged just enough to pull her head back so he could nip at the soft skin under her jaw. "Seriously, I eighty percent mean it."

"Oh, I'm going to take you home," he promised. "But what brings you into the locker room in this sexy dress with those curves and those legs and the heels?"

"I was out with a girlfriend. Every couple of months we splurge and go to this really trendy, upscale place that makes the best dirty martinis, and to make it extra fun, we dress up." She cupped the side of his face in her hand. "But I should have been here tonight and I felt shitty about it. I grabbed a Lyft and got here in time to see the last few minutes, and then I figured I might as well wait for you. And wait, and wait."

"It's kind of my thing. I like to decompress and let all the adrenaline and emotions of the game and shit work through my system before I shower and head out." Her brow furrowed as she looked at him thoughtfully, so he shrugged. "Every guy has his own thing. Some guys want to dissect every second on the ice. Some want to leave it behind until it's time to focus on it again."

She nodded. "The Burkes don't leave anything behind. My dad and Erik are pretty intense guys."

"I've heard that about them." He skimmed his hands up

the back of her thighs and then under her dress to cup her ass. "You're pretty intense yourself."

"Okay, Lecroix. Hit the shower so we can get out of here. I'll wait in the hall." She stepped backward, as if to move out of his reach, but he snagged her hand.

"I won't be long." He leaned in to kiss her, doing his best to keep from brushing his body against her dress. "And for the record, I didn't expect you to come tonight because I know how you feel about hockey, so don't feel shitty about going out instead."

She smiled and kissed him again before walking out of the locker room, so he didn't regret saying it, even if it wasn't totally the truth. He didn't want her to feel shitty about skipping the game, so that part was true. But it would have been cool to have her there—to have known she was in the crowd cheering for him.

Earlier in the night, he'd told himself it was a good thing she'd opted out. It was a good reminder that all of this was temporary and it didn't matter if she was willing to sit through a hockey game or not because when he left Boston behind, he'd be leaving her behind, too.

And that thought had done absolutely nothing to cheer him up.

11

One of Kristen's least favorite times of day was the fifteen minutes or so she spent in Stan's office every morning, reviewing anything outstanding from the day before and strategizing current tasks and appointments.

When there was a closed door between them, she was usually able to shove her personal dislike of the man to the back of her mind and focus on the work. But when she was sitting across from him, with nothing but his pretentious walnut desk between them, it was a lot harder to ignore him.

"One more thing," he said when she closed her notebook and started to get up.

"Okay." She lowered herself into the chair again, wondering if he was finally going to give her the promotion. If, *finally*, he was going to acknowledge that she worked her ass off for him and show some gratitude.

That wasn't likely, she knew, but she didn't need the words. She just wanted the promotion. Not only was it time, but it was long past due.

"This relationship of yours, with that hockey player...I've been thinking about that." He paused, giving her a look that made his distaste for the situation clear. "How serious is it, exactly?"

Kristen gave herself a moment to consider her answer before speaking. While he didn't seem to approve of hockey players, he *was* a fan of stable and respectable relationships. But she knew she was walking a fine line, too, because if this man thought she was going to be distracted by wedding planning and then babies in the near future, he might pass her over for the promotion on those grounds.

Why the hell she couldn't get the promotion she'd earned based on nothing but her exemplary job performance was something she couldn't think about right now or she'd do or say something she'd regret.

"I'm not sure he's as serious about our future as I am. Was," she said quietly. Since she and Will would go their separate ways in the future anyway—and holy crap, did *that* hurt to think about—and her boss was already biased against him, she might as well lay the groundwork for the end of her relationship. She'd also be putting to rest any concerns he had about her ability to focus wholly on work in the near future.

"It's probably for the best," he said, not exactly oozing sympathy. "I mean, athletes can be attractive and wealthy, which appeals to a certain kind of woman, I'm sure, but the lifestyle...I expected you to have higher standards."

No. Not just no, but *oh, hell no.*

Standing up seemed to happen without her intending to, as if her body realized before her brain that she couldn't do this anymore. She couldn't keep selling herself out in the hope of working her way up to a job she could barely stomach.

She was so done with this judgmental asshole, and he could shove his promotion up his ass. "With all due respect, Stan—which is absolutely no respect, by the way—you can go fuck yourself."

She took great satisfaction in watching him gape and gasp—except for the few seconds he clutched his throat and she was afraid she'd killed him—before he started spluttering. "I beg your pardon?"

"I quit. Effective"—she looked at her watch and then back at him—"now."

Before he could turn his strangled sounds of outrage into words, Kristen turned on her heel and walked out of his office, pulling the door closed behind her with enthusiasm.

She went immediately to her office and started gathering the few personal belongings she kept there. They all fit in her tote—her favorite pen and coffee mug, along with a framed picture of Erik she'd taken herself when he was in a sweater and jeans, and it was one of the very few photos of him out of his hockey gear.

Annie popped her head in. "What's going on? Why are you packing?"

"I'm done."

"No, you can't be done. If you just calm down a bit and—"

"I told Stan to go fuck himself."

"Oh. Yeah, you're done." Annie stepped fully into the office and closed the door behind her. "We have so many contacts and you're freaking awesome, so you'll get a new job in like seconds, but I'm going to miss having you here."

"I'll miss you, too. The rest of it? Not so much." She couldn't find anything else she was taking with her, so she gave her friend a hug. "We'll get together in the next few days, okay? But right now, I'm walking out of here."

There were a few other people she said goodbye to on her way out, but judging by the ripple of conversation through the office, Stan was recovering from the shock and the shit was about to hit the fan.

In the elevator, the emotions started rolling through her, though. Anger at Stan, though that was familiar enough. The realization and accompanying horror at finding herself suddenly unemployed, and in such a way that wasn't going to garner a great reference, to say the least.

And utter disgust that she'd wasted so many years of putting up with Stan's shit because the job was a part of her journey, not her destination, only to blow it all up and derail everything in a fit of temper.

But, really, he was a dickhead, and it was a miracle she'd put up with it as long as she had.

There was a possibility that promotion was never going to come, she admitted to herself. If Stan couldn't value her when was giving almost everything to the job, he wasn't going to value her in the future. Eventually she was going to meet a guy and finally feel the urge to settle down and start a family. And Stan knew that.

By the time she stepped into her apartment and closed the door behind her, she'd experienced the full range of emotions several times each, and she was exhausted.

She wanted Will.

As shitty as her day was, all she wanted right now was to climb onto Will's lap and let him wrap his arms around her. It wouldn't help her situation any, but for a few minutes, she'd be able to let everything go and just feel warm and safe and cared for.

She actually had their existing text chain pulled up on her phone screen, with her thumb ready to type, when she caught herself.

He had practice today, and they were preparing for a road game tomorrow. They played regionally, and it was a matinee game to benefit a local fundraiser, so he wouldn't be gone overnight, but it didn't matter. He had hockey to worry about, not letting Kristen cry tears of disappointment and frustration into his shirt.

Maybe if he was an accountant or sold cars or fixed people's plumbing, she would have sent the text. But she knew that being a professional athlete at Erik and Will's level wasn't about the hour of regulation gameplay. Practice and strategy. Films. Focus. Dedication.

There was nothing he could do. She'd already quit, and the next steps were updating her resume and reaching out to some of the contacts she'd made over the years.

She wasn't going to break Will's focus because she needed a hug.

WILL STEPPED UP BEHIND KRISTEN, who'd been washing the same wine glass for at least two minutes, and kissed her neck as he wrapped his arms around her waist. "Are we celebrating or mourning or raging or what?"

"I don't really know." She rinsed the glass and set it upside down on the drying mat. "I'm doing all three at the same time, I think."

"That sounds exhausting."

"Two glasses of wine didn't help." She leaned back against him, and he felt her relax a little in his arms.

"You could have texted me instead of waiting until I got here to tell me. I would have been here earlier."

"Yeah, like you leaving the ice because I had a bad day at work is a thing that should have happened."

Will heard the old wounds under the sarcasm and turned her to face him, tipping her chin up. "You didn't just have a bad day at work. I know how hard you've been working for that promotion and toward your end goal and, even though you made the right decision for yourself, it has to be devastating. And when your world gets rocked like that, you can call me and I'll be here for you."

She made a face that told him she'd go along with the sentiment, even if she wouldn't allow herself to believe it.

He cursed Lamont Burke, though he didn't dare say the words aloud. And maybe she was right not to believe him. Would he have skipped out early if she'd called him? Probably, unless it was an actual game situation. It had to have been a huge emotional blow for her.

But he shouldn't be promising that she could call him and he'd be there because it wasn't a promise he'd be able to keep very much longer. When he was with Kristen now, he felt the same kind of urgency he felt in the final minutes of a hockey game. Time was running out.

"At least I was smart enough to buy ice cream when I went shopping yesterday," she said, giving him the first genuine smile of the night. "So I can drown out my sorrows with mint chocolate chip and a funny movie."

"Sounds perfect." He kissed the back of her neck again, smiling against her skin when she shivered. "You ready for it now?"

"You scoop while I go wash away my self-pity and throw on some movie-watching pj's."

He slapped her on the ass as she walked past him and laughed at the saucy look she threw over her shoulder. Then he pulled open her freezer drawer and couldn't help smiling. Next to her mint chocolate chip was a carton of maple walnut ice cream.

It was a small thing on the surface, maybe, but it was just another way she really *saw* him and made him feel important. And the first thing he'd thought when she told him she'd quit her job ran through his head again, resurfacing despite his resolve not to go there.

She was free to go to Baltimore with him.

It was there now, in his head again, and he couldn't stop thinking about it. That hadn't been part of the deal. The dating was supposed to be fake—a relationship made up to keep people from dragging Kristen's name through the dirt —but it had stopped being fake for him. He wasn't sure exactly when, but what he felt for Kristen was real.

He was in love with her.

The arguments were all there. It was too soon—*way* too soon. She hated hockey, which was a huge part of his life. She was a complete stranger to his family, and her family wouldn't shed a tear if he got hit by a bus.

All of that was true, and none of it put a dent in the truth. He'd been sent to Boston, chose a place to eat based on the grilled chicken, and met a strong, amazing, sexy woman who changed everything. And he couldn't stay here, but he didn't want to go home without her.

By the time he'd scooped them each a dish of ice cream and carried it into the living room, he had his emotions mostly under control again. He wasn't going to be able to put them totally in a box—he was too shaken for that—but he didn't want her to read his thoughts on his face. Not yet, anyway.

"Perfect timing," he heard her say as he set the bowls on the coffee table.

He gave himself a few more seconds of trying to shove his feelings in a box for later before he looked up. Her movie-watching pajamas were a long-sleeved thermal top that had been washed so many times, it barely had any pink left to it, and flannel sleep pants with unicorns on them.

"Thank you for the maple walnut," he said, and she paused for a kiss he was only too happy to give her before picking up her bowl and settling onto the couch.

He sat next to her, in the corner, and he smiled when she settled against him. She had the remote control and flipped through the channels until she found an old eighties comedy they both found ridiculous but also funny. After tossing the remote on the table, she dug into her ice cream.

But with the first bite of his maple walnut, he felt that clock ticking down again. The standard conditioning stint was almost over, and he felt good. The Harriers weren't going to try to get him an extension, and he knew he should at least bring it up. It had to be talked about, if only so he'd know if she felt the same way he did.

She'd made room in her freezer for his favorite ice cream, even though she thought it was disgusting. That had to mean something. Or maybe he was reading too much into it, hoping for signs she might be falling for him as hard as he'd fallen for her.

But not tonight, he decided. She'd had a spectacularly shitty day and right now she needed ice cream and laughter. It wasn't the time for a deep, emotional discussion. And if she didn't feel the same he did, he'd probably have to leave to hide the hurt, and he didn't want her to be alone.

So he'd eat ice cream, watch a dumb comedy, and then take her to bed. There was still a little time left on the clock.

THERE WERE VERY few woes that that couldn't be cured by ice

cream, a movie, and multiple orgasms, Kristen thought as she skimmed her fingernails over the sheen of sweat on Will's naked back. She was almost breathing normally again, and her muscles were so relaxed, she wasn't sure she'd ever move again.

Not that she wanted to right now. She loved the weight of his body on hers, and she smiled as he lifted his head from her shoulder to kiss it and then her mouth.

Then he looked at her, his mouth curved in a smile that was so sweet, she sighed and stroked his hair back from his forehead. At this moment, she didn't care what happened beyond her apartment. Nothing else really mattered because all she needed was this man, who she had somehow fallen so fast and so hard in love with, looking at her the way he was right now.

And this man loved her, too.

It was there on his face—in his eyes—and she couldn't look away.

Will was the man who would love her for the rest of her life. Her Prince Charming. Her knight in shining armor. He would hold her hair and rub her back when she was sick, and bring home champagne when she had something to celebrate. He wouldn't hold her back or slow her down, but he would be at her side forever—his hand at the small of her back to reassure, comfort, or encourage.

Until the ice called, she reminded herself. He might love her, but he had a life and a team waiting for him in Baltimore, and when push came to shove, he would love hockey more. She knew the drill—she'd lived it her entire life—and she wouldn't try to change his mind. He wouldn't stay, and hearing him actually say the words out loud would hurt more than just knowing them in her heart.

A tear slid down from the corner of her eye, running toward her temple before she could blink it away. Will wiped it away with his thumb, his brow furrowing slightly.

Before he could speak—maybe saying something that would change their lives—she buried her fingers in his hair and pulled his head down so she could kiss him.

Sixteen hours later, the ice called, and it all fell apart.

She could see it on Will's face as soon as he walked through the door after a road game she knew they'd won. He had something to say that she wasn't going to like, and she knew before he opened his mouth it would have to do with hockey.

"What's up?" she asked when he looked reluctant to say what was on his mind. "Just say it."

"There's been a lot of talking—the team doctors and physical therapists and, hell, everybody in the Harriers organization, it feels like—and we're not going to try to extend my conditioning stint with the commissioner. They feel like I'm ready to rejoin the team in Baltimore."

And that was it, Kristen thought. It didn't matter how much love for her she saw in his eyes. Hockey summoned, and he was leaving.

"Congratulations," she forced herself to say, knowing how brittle the smile she forced was. "When do you leave?"

"I fly back in the morning."

"That's...soon." She felt weak, as if her muscles were losing their ability to hold her upright, but she tried to focus on not letting it show. She sat on the couch, though, just in case her knees gave out. "They'll be glad to have you back."

"Yeah," he said, sitting on the other end. In *his* corner, she thought. He had a designated corner of the couch. His own ice cream in the freezer. "So, we should talk about this."

"What's to talk about?" She lifted her chin, knowing pretense was the only way she could get through this. "The story's over."

"It doesn't have to be."

He said that now, while he was sitting in her living room with her, but as soon as his plane landed in Baltimore, his focus would shift to the Harriers and helping his team make up the ground they'd lost while he was out.

"That idiot and his *Hometown Hoser* piece have been old news for a while now, Kristen. The real story—*our* story— doesn't have be over."

"I don't date hockey players," she said with absolutely no conviction in her voice.

He laughed. "I'm not buying that. You've been dating a hockey player."

"Was." She looked away. "Past tense. I blew up my promotion, and the hockey blogs will all be talking about your big return to the Harriers, so it seems pretty over to me."

His expression hardened, but she could see the truth in his eyes. He was hurting, too, though not enough to stay. Then he took a deep breath and reached across the cushion between them to put his hand over hers.

"Come to Baltimore with me."

The words fell between them, and it seemed to Kristen as if neither of them even breathed for several seconds.

"Come with me," he said again.

"I can't do that," she said, shaking her head.

"Why not? You're between jobs right now. Just come with me."

"And do what? Sit alone in *your* home, waiting for you?"

"I've been here every night with you," he pointed out,

but she could barely hear him over the pounding of her heart and the voice in her head telling her she'd been right all along.

Hockey always wins.

"You and I both know it'll be different when you're back with the Harriers. And you'll be going extra hard to prove your shoulder's better and to try to make up lost ground in the standings."

He didn't deny it. "That doesn't mean there's no room in my life for you."

"We've been so happy," she whispered. "Why can't you just stay here? Hang up your skates and we can make a life together."

He looked shocked that she'd suggest such a thing, which didn't surprise her. "I can't go out like this."

"What do you mean? You've been playing a long time. You've hoisted the Cup more than once. You've also taken a beating. Nobody would be surprised if you decide it's time to retire."

"If I retire now, it looks like I went down and couldn't make it back."

"So what?"

He recoiled as if she'd struck him. "*So what?* How can you say that to me?"

"Your career speaks for itself, Will. What could you possibly have left to prove to anybody?"

"I *don't* have anything to prove. To anybody." She winced because there was probably some subtext in that statement aimed at her. "I love playing this game, and I'm going to play it as long as I can. I'm not ready to retire because I'm simply not done yet."

"Then go," she said, amazed at how calm her voice sounded when she was shattering on the inside.

"Kristen, don't do this. Please."

"I spent my whole childhood waiting for scraps of attention from my own father and brother. I won't do it anymore."

"Scraps?" He stood, shaking his head. "That's bullshit, Kristen. You're not being fair."

"It's how I feel."

"You always knew I was going back to Baltimore," he said as she stood, not wanting him looming over her. "I never gave you any reason to believe I wouldn't."

"I...sometimes things change." She couldn't bring herself to admit she'd fallen in love with him and had hoped he would love her enough to choose her.

"What hasn't changed is that I've worked for months to rehab my shoulder so I could get back out on the ice. I didn't see this coming, and it *does* change things. But not enough that I'll just turn my back on my team and my career like that."

"Then nothing really changed at all." She was going to break down soon. She could feel it building in her, like the tide pulling away before the tsunami crashed over her. And she didn't want him to be here when the big wave hit. "Go, Will. Don't make it harder."

His jaw flexed, and his hands were clenched, but after a few excruciating seconds, he exhaled slowly. "We're not going to get anywhere like this. I have to go, Kristen. I can't *not* go back. But we're not done."

Her throat had tightened beyond the ability for her to speak, so she watched him in silence as he put his coat and boots on and yanked open her door. But he turned back a final time, giving her a long look filled with raw emotion. "We are *not* done."

As soon as the door closed behind him, she sank to the

couch and flopped over on her side, sobs wracking her body. It didn't matter what he said, because he was still leaving.

And they were done.

12

W ill woke up in his own bed, and his first thought was of Kristen. His last thought as he fell asleep was of Kristen. And he'd thought about her almost every minute between. Waking up after almost no sleep in his hotel room. The plane ride home. Walking into his condo.

He'd been haunted by her—by the pain that was all he could feel right now. He'd sent her several text messages and left her two voicemails. She hadn't responded, which only cut deeper.

It was tempting to believe he hadn't meant anything to her after all, but he knew that would be a lie. She was in love with him. She just couldn't get past the resentments of her childhood and the damage Lamont Burke had done.

Today, he was rejoining his team. A full practice. A final check-in for his shoulder. Tomorrow, a home game. He was back.

And it felt empty. *He* felt empty.

A few hours later, he sat on the bench and, after rehydrating, watched the second line do their thing. Physically, he was in damn good shape. His shoulder was good, and the time in Boston had gotten his legs back under him. There was no reason he wouldn't be 100 percent for tomorrow's game.

Mitchell, who'd been the left wing to his right wing for several years, sat next to him. "You're playing pretty hard for a practice. Got something to prove?"

What he had was a lot of emotional turmoil he didn't know what to do with, but he shouldn't be bringing it out on the ice with him. Definitely not with his teammates, but not with their opponents tomorrow, either. The last thing he wanted to do was make sloppy mistakes or lose his shit and accidentally hurt somebody.

"Just glad to be back," he said, since Mitchell was his teammate, not his therapist.

"How are things going with Burke's sister?" Mitchell shook his head and didn't wait for an answer. "Did *not* see that one coming, man. Can't lie."

"I don't know," he lied, because he didn't want to get into it today. Or ever, really, though at some point it would have to be said, and it would have to be before Erik Burke rolled into town. But not today. "I'm not sure it'll survive the distance."

"That's tough, man. Hopefully Burke will be a professional about it and leave that shit off the ice, where it belongs."

Will nodded, but he didn't really care. Burke could high stick him, take him to the ground, and beat him bloody on the ice—it still wouldn't hurt him as much as Kristen had.

He knew what to do with the physical injuries. Grit his teeth and play through the pain. Ice. Heat. Very carefully monitored pain meds when necessary. Hot tubs and massages. Sometimes, like the shoulder, they could only be waited out.

But he had no idea what do with a fucking broken heart. Based on how he felt right now, none of the broken hearts he thought he'd suffered in his younger days had been the real thing, and he had no coping skills for it.

He did his best to keep himself in check for the remainder of practice. He did everything right. He cleared his final medical checkup with the team doctor. But he still couldn't feel the rush of triumph at a successful return from injury.

He showered then texted Kristen and got no response. He ate a meal because he had to. He stared at the television for a while because he had nothing else to do, and then he went to bed at the same time he always went to bed before a game, but he stared at the ceiling.

He went to sleep thinking of Kristen and woke again thinking of her. He felt stuck in some kind of dark, emotional *Groundhog Day* situation, and it sucked. But he got up and showered.

Tonight he'd be in front of the Harriers hometown crowd, and they were going to be screaming his name. He owed it to them and to his team to put Kristen out of his mind somehow—if it was even possible—and give it everything he had.

It was time to suck it up and do his job.

KRISTEN GLANCED at her phone when it chimed, but chose to ignore it when she saw Erik's name on the screen. She didn't want to talk to her brother. She didn't want to talk to *anybody*, though she was going to have to get over that pretty quickly if she wanted to find a new job so she could continue to eat.

Thanks to her savings, she wasn't in crisis mode yet, so she was giving herself time to wallow—three days so far. It annoyed her to even *be* wallowing, since she'd known long before she even met Will that she couldn't compete with hockey. The game came first, always. But since she was sad, she was allowing herself to go all in on the wallow, which included avoiding people who might try to help her feel better, like her brother.

When she heard a key in the lock, she groaned and dropped her head against the back of the couch. She really should take Erik's key away from him.

"You *are* home," he said after he'd let himself in. He kicked off his boots and hung his coat up. "I wasn't sure, since you won't answer my text messages or answer my calls."

"What are you doing here?"

"We just got back from Montreal, and Dad's been sending me text messages about you. I figured if you were bad enough so he not only noticed but is worried, it must be bad. And the more you ignored me, the more worried I got."

"I'm fine. Go away. You must have game tapes to watch or something."

"I'm not leaving you like this, Kris."

"Like what? Sitting in my own damn apartment, watching some television and relaxing?"

"Yeah, I hate to point it out, but the TV's not even on. And you're in your bad-day sweatpants with your bad-day hair."

She actually laughed, which she hadn't done in days. "Bad-day hair?"

"You wear ratty sweatpants and just ball your hair up in

one of those puffy elastic things when you're having a shitty day." He dropped into the chair. "Also you have red eyes and a red nose, and your face is so puffy you look like you're having an allergic reaction to something."

"It warms my heart you could take the time out of your day to stop by and cheer me up," she said, tossing a coaster at his head. Of course he had great reflexes and ducked his head easily to the side to avoid it.

Fucking hockey players.

"Talk to me," he said. She ignored him, but he just settled himself a little deeper in the chair and folded his arms. "I'm not leaving here until you do."

"You'll leave eventually. You have practice. Games. Workouts. Whatever it is. You'll have to do something hockey-related. You always do."

"So this is about Cross." He rolled his eyes. "Or Will. Whatever you want to call him."

Hearing his name cut through the numbness that had taken over Kristen once she'd smashed some things in anger and then cried herself out. Being numb had been working out for her so far, but apparently that was over.

"Maybe I'm sitting here in my bad day sweatpants, apparently *not* watching television, because I not only blew up my promotion but also quit my job."

"*Maybe* don't forget you're talking to your brother here. I know you, and this isn't how you'd deal with losing your job, no matter how focused you were on that promotion. Like I said, when even Dad—"

"I don't want to hear about Dad right now," she yelled, tossing a throw pillow at him. He dodged that, too. "I don't want to hear about hockey at all, but I definitely don't want to hear about the asshole who's probably only concerned about his daughter because whatever's bothering her might be something that would distract his son from his game."

"Have you heard from Cross?" She noticed he didn't bother denying it.

"A couple of voicemails and a few text messages. He misses me." And missing him was so hard, she wasn't sure she'd ever fully live her life again. It felt empty without him.

"Isn't that a good thing?"

"No," she snapped. "Because he doesn't miss me *enough*, does he?"

"He's got a job to do, though. A career, and a team that depends on him. Just because he has to be in Baltimore doesn't mean it has to be over."

"If you're going to sound like Dad and try to explain why hockey is more important than me but not to worry because I still matter even if I don't feel like I do, don't let the door hit you in the ass on the way out."

"Here's the thing, though, Kris. Hockey didn't make Dad an asshole. He's...just an asshole." He held up his hand. "Yes, I know he and I are close. I love the guy, and I appreciate everything he's done for me, but that doesn't mean I can't see how he's wired. It's a shitty thing to say out loud, but even if I sucked at sports, he was always going to put me above you. Because you're a girl."

He wasn't wrong, and Kristen blew out a sharp breath. "I've about had my fill of misogynistic douchebags."

"Hockey's my life, and Dad made it his life, too. It sucks we made it your life, too, but that's not the game's fault. That's Dad and, yes, me. Maybe if Mom..."

He let the words trail away, and Kristen didn't bother to rebut them. They both knew it wouldn't have mattered if their mother hadn't died. Lamont hadn't valued his wife's opinion any more than he valued his daughter's.

"It almost sounds like you *want* me to end up with the infamous Cross Lecroix," she joked, hoping to lighten the mood even if she didn't feel it. Her brother wasn't going to leave until he thought she'd be okay, so she needed to pretend to be okay if she wanted to get back to staring at the blank TV screen.

Erik didn't even smile. "I hate that fucking guy, but when you were with him, you were the happiest I've ever seen you. There was nothing fake about that."

"No," she admitted in a quiet voice. "There was nothing fake about my feelings for him."

"I'm pretty sure he wasn't faking, either." She shook her head. "So, what happened?"

"Hockey happened." She sighed and picked at her nail polish. There wasn't much left of it. "Hockey *always* happens."

"What does that mean, exactly? You didn't even know he played hockey when you first hooked up, but you knew before you started feeling shit for him." He paused, giving her a hard look. "Tell me you didn't give him an ultimatum."

"It's not out of the question for a guy his age, who's accomplished what he has, to consider retiring."

"Kris." He shook his head. "A guy with a career like his isn't going to retire when he's at a low point. He's going to wait until he's back at full strength—maybe even make another run at the Cup before he hangs up his skates, or it'll just look like he couldn't make it back."

"That's what he said."

"And you framed it as a choice between you and his career?"

"I don't want to hear it," Kristen snapped, her patience for the conversation at an end. "Of course you'll support him choosing his career since you chose yours over Andie, and she didn't even ask you to retire. She just wanted you to make time for her when you weren't on the ice."

When some of the color drained from Erik's face and his jaw clenched, guilt drowned out her anger. "I'm sorry, Erik."

It had been almost three months since the woman Kristen had honestly believed would be her sister-in-law someday had gotten sick of fighting for Erik's attention and walked away. And Lamont hadn't helped. He fought against anything that distracted his son, and he wasn't happy unless Erik was preparing for a game, playing a game, or analyzing everything he'd done wrong in a game in order to be ready for the next game.

"You want to keep it *that* real, Kris? I don't think Cross chose hockey over you. *You* chose it for him. You told yourself the entire time you were with him that he would eventually choose the game over you, so you wouldn't even listen to him unless he said he'd quit."

"Fuck you."

"Have you responded to his text messages?" He leaned forward in the chair when she clenched her jaw and refused to answer. "I didn't think so. You boxed him into a corner and when he wasn't willing to just drop everything—to walk away from his team, his contract, and his fucking future Hall-of-Fame career—just because you like having him around, you told yourself you were right all along and shoved him out the door."

"I wanted to be *first*," she yelled, and she stood as the anger swelled to drown out the sorrow again. "I wanted to be more important to him than hockey."

Erik stood too, taking a step toward her. "Did you tell him you're in love with him?"

She bit into her bottom lip, trying to keep it from trembling, as tears spilled over her heated cheeks. Dammit, she wasn't all cried out after all. Her throat was so tight, she wasn't sure she could talk, so she just shook her head.

He wrapped his arms around her, holding tight, and for a few moments she just listened to her brother's heartbeat and let the rhythm of his breathing calm her.

"You need to tell him," he said quietly, with his cheek resting on top of her bad-day hair bun.

"It's too late." She buried her face against his chest, wishing for things it was definitely too late to be wishing for.

"You better not be wiping your nose on my shirt. And it's not too late. He's still reaching out, Kris. You need to be willing to reach out, too. To compromise. As much as it kills me to admit it, he and I are both looking at a few more years at the most. You're going to give up a lifetime of love with him because of a few years of hockey and travel? He's in Baltimore, not California. It's like an hour and a half flight. Or you move to Baltimore for a few years. You can make it work if he's worth it. And he'll make it work because he *knows* you're worth it."

"Or maybe he could get traded to the Marauders," she added.

She actually felt his full-body shudder. "I'll miss you when you move to Baltimore, sis."

Laughing, she backed out of his arms, using the sleeves of her baggy sweatshirt to mop at her face. "I don't know, Erik."

"This whole *hockey or me* thing? That's your damage, Kris—done by Dad and by me—not his. Don't put Cross in that box with us without giving him a chance to prove he can love you *and* play the game." The muscles along his jaw flexed a few times, and she thought she glimpsed a sheen of moisture in his eyes before he blinked. "Give it a chance,

Kris. Trust me, you'll always be sorry if you slam that door without even trying."

Andie. The sadness and regret was clear in Erik's eyes, and Kristen was sorry she'd brought her into the conversation. But her brother kept his emotions so locked down as a rule, she hadn't realized until now just how sorry he was he let Andie walk away.

"Has he reached out to you *today*?" Erik asked, and she nodded, even though she didn't see the significance. "Yeah, so he's preparing to go out on his home ice tonight for the first time in months, and he has to prove he's back to a hundred percent against a team with a bad habit of teeing off on opponents' known weak spots, but he's thinking about you. Reaching out to you because you're what's on his mind. That means something, Kris."

She nodded, glancing at her phone where Will's texts and voicemails waited, unanswered. "I'll think about it."

"Think about it in the shower," he suggested, and the exaggerated wrinkling of his nose made her laugh.

He left a few minutes later, after she promised to clean herself up and eat a proper meal since the empty Little Debbie wrappers littering the coffee table had ratted her out.

But she didn't get in the shower after he left. Instead, she returned to the couch and picked up her phone. She didn't feel strong enough to hear Will's voice at the moment, so she didn't listen to the voicemail. Instead, she pulled up the text messages and read through them.

Then she took a deep breath and finally responded.

I miss you, too. Have a good game tonight.

There was no response, not even the little dots to tell her he was typing, and she looked at the clock and realized he had to be in the locker room, gearing up and going through whatever pregame rituals he had because it was almost game time.

She was halfway to the shower when it chimed.

Thanks. I'll call you tomorrow. Please answer.

"Cross, the Marauders are on your schedule for next week. Do you think your relationship with his sister will have any effect on the rivalry between you and Erik Burke?"

Will swiped sweat from his forehead, using the motion of his arm to hide the flash of emotion he was sure had to show on his face. They'd just won their second game since his return, and the media still wanted to talk about Kristen, who he hadn't heard from since her text last night. He locked his feelings down because he'd known this question would come, and he'd rehearsed his answer for it until he could say the words without emotion.

"Burke and I will do what we've always done," he said in a flat voice. "We're both out there to get the win, and that's what we'll be focused on next week."

He'd tried to call Kristen three times before tonight's game, and she hadn't answered. That had hurt even more than the unanswered text messages and voicemails, because she'd given him hope. She said she missed him, too. So he'd spent the rest of the night and most of today hoping she'd missed him enough to answer when he called, but apparently not.

"Do you think Kristen will be at your game against the Marauders? Will she have to choose between her brother's team and the Harriers?"

"She's pretty busy, and we haven't had a chance to talk about it." He gave the man behind the microphone a terse smile. "Are we done here, or do you have more questions about how we played tonight?"

"How's the shoulder?"

"It's solid, and it won't be a concern going forward."

There were a few more inane questions before he was able to escape and head for the locker room. Instead of lingering and clearing his head as he'd done for pretty much his entire career, he hit the showers and got dressed in record time.

He was going to try one more time. He'd call, and if she sent him to voicemail, he was going to let her go. But he didn't want to call her from the locker room or his car, so he needed to get home.

Several years after he signed with the Harriers and had earned himself a sense of job security, he'd invested in a condo close enough to the water to be overpriced but too far away to have a decent view. But he'd liked the neighborhood and the secured entrance. It was pretty unassuming on the outside, but the units inside were nice, and it worked for him.

He was driving past his building to turn the corner toward a shared parking garage when he noticed somebody —and it looked like a woman—sitting on the front steps, which was odd. There was a courtyard behind the building where residents could sit outside in comfort, rather than on brick stairs.

Then the woman lifted her head, watching as he drove by, and he slammed on the brakes.

Kristen.

He pulled the car to the side of the road with one tire on the curb and killed the engine. He could park it later. Or they could tow it. He didn't really care.

Kristen stood as he walked up the sidewalk, brushing off

the seat of her jeans, and he didn't stop until he could reach out and pull her into his embrace. Her arms wrapped around his waist, and he squeezed her, inhaling the scent of her hair.

He didn't know why she was there yet, but he didn't care. She was here, and it was enough for a few minutes.

"I saw several missed calls from you when the plane landed," she said into his coat, and he had to pull back a bit so he could hear her. "I was going to call you back, but I knew you had a game again tonight, and I didn't want to talk to you on the phone anyway."

"Let's go inside. Do you have a bag?"

"I got a hotel room," she said, wiping a few stray tears from her eyes. "I wasn't sure...I didn't want to be sitting on your front step with luggage. Also, there's a young woman in the Harriers office whose name I didn't catch, and you can't be mad at her. I told her who I was and that I was trying to surprise you but must have accidentally deleted the text with your address."

"I'll buy her flowers."

"I think just not having her fired would be enough," she said, and for the first time since he'd walked out of her apartment, he laughed.

He didn't let go of her hand as he punched in the entrance code or in the elevator, and he didn't let go of her while he unlocked his door and had the virtual gadget turn his lights on.

"Oh, that's weird," Kristen said, stopping inside the front door. "Your apartment is decorated a lot like mine, except your furniture is a lot newer. And probably a lot more expensive."

"Décor compatibility gets added to the list, somewhere after sex compatibility and pizza compatibility." She chuckled, but he could feel the nervous tension in her, and he squeezed her hand. "Take your coat off. I don't have any alcohol in the house, but do you want some water or coffee or anything? I think I bought orange juice."

"No, I'm good." She pulled her hand free and turned to face him. "I came so we could talk. I realize now I had a really knee-jerk reaction to you leaving that came from my shit and wasn't fair to you."

"I shouldn't have left. I should have tried to talk through it instead of walking out."

"I don't know that I would have listened, then. Erik told me I'd already made up my mind that you'd choose hockey over me and that I never actually gave you that choice."

"He's not quite as much of an asshole as I've always thought," he had to concede, however grudgingly. "And, you know, it felt good being back on my home ice, with the crowd chanting my name. Both games were tough and we won them both, but it didn't feel the same. I know what it cost me to play, and the price was too much."

"Will, I—"

"I love you, Kristen. And you tell me what you need from me, and I'll do it."

"It doesn't work that way."

"Sure it does. You tell me what I have to do to keep you for the rest of my life, and I'll do it. It's that simple." His jaw clenched for a second before he swallowed hard. "If you want me to retire—to walk away from hockey—then I'll tell my team tomorrow and make the announcement as soon as they give me the okay because my heart's not in it and won't ever be again if I have to give you up."

"You can't do that."

"Yes, I can. You're saying it doesn't work that way and I

can't do that, and I'm telling you absolutely it does and I can."

"And then what? What are you going to do if you don't play hockey?"

"Dust off that business degree? And I'll eat more carbs. Refuse to ever do another front barbell squat. Enjoy the entire holiday season. Not give a shit how much I weigh. Soak in hot tubs because I want to and not because I have to. Then I'll eat even *more* carbs." He moved slowly toward her, his eyes locked on her face. "Most importantly, I'll go to bed with you. I'll make love to you, and then I'll wake up beside you. Every day, for the rest of our lives."

"Promising carbs and sex isn't even fair, you know."

"Are you still going to love me when I've been stuffing my face with carbs and stopped doing front barbell squats?"

She trailed her finger over his chest and down his rippled abs. "I think you'll have to eat a lot of carbs before you can't open my pickle jars anymore."

He chuckled. "I can't figure out if that's a euphemism of some kind or not."

"Maybe." She shrugged. "But also maybe not. But I do know I'll still love you when you can't open my pickle jars, either literally *or* metaphorically."

He bent his head to kiss her, but she put her hand on his chest and pushed him away. Frowning, he took a step back. "What's the matter?"

"I'm not letting you retire, Will. That's not what I came here for, and it's not what I want."

Fear shot through him. She had just said she'd *still* love him, so she *did* love him now. What had she come here for if not to work things out between them?

"I have some issues from growing up a Burke, to put it lightly," she continued. "They're old wounds I thought had hardened, but falling in love with you made me so vulnerable, I was too busy trying to keep those walls intact to see I didn't need them. You're not like my family. You're *especially* not like my dad, and I think if I ever truly believed you were, I would have walked away. But I panicked and just had this need for you prove you cared about me more than you care about hockey."

"I *love* you," he said, looking directly into her pretty blue eyes. "I mean, I love hockey, too, but it's my job. It's not the same."

"In my family, that kind of love *is* the same. But that's on me, not you. I *know* you love me." He watched her blink away tears, feeling a little choked up himself. This wasn't easy for her. "I believe that, in my heart. And hockey is a part of you, and I love you. *All* of you."

"You have to be sure, Kristen, because what we just went through? I can't do it again."

"I am absolutely sure. I know there will be times your focus is on the game, and times when your travel schedule might be inconvenient, but I'll remind myself that it's not a choice between me and the game. And I have to compromise, too. We'll do it together."

"I like the sound of *together*." He caressed the side of her face with his thumb. "And maybe, if you let a little bit of hockey in, you can meet some people. There are a whole lot of hockey players out there with beautiful families they love very much. We can make this work because we love each other, and we'll figure it all out. Together."

"Do you think Baltimore will hate me as much as Boston hates you?"

He laughed, pulling her toward the couch so they could sit down. "No, they won't. Your brother? Yes. But they'll love you because I do. And you don't have to move to Baltimore, you know. I know you'll want to keep your apartment. We can bounce back and forth between your place and mine. If you find a great job in Boston, then I'll have to be away a little more during the season, but it'll only be for a few years."

She turned toward him instead of sitting, and then cupped his face in her hands. "We'll figure all that out. For now, just know that I love you and I'm always going to love you."

"I love you, too." He kissed her again, holding nothing back as he let the pain and loss of their separation go and simply rejoiced at having her in his arms again.

When he ended the kiss and stroked her hair away from her face, her eyes sparkled. "Who would have thought I'd end up married to a hockey player?"

His pulse quickened in response, and he grinned. "Are you proposing to me, Kristen Burke?"

"I'm not very good at waiting for a man to make the first move, I guess."

"I do like that about you. And yes, I want to marry you. I want that more than anything."

"We're going to make a great team," she whispered, right before he kissed her again.

EPILOGUE

T *hanksgiving, almost ten months later...*

"ANOTHER FACE-OFF IN A NEUTRAL ZONE."

Kristen laughed as Will stepped aside to hold the door to the restaurant open for her. "We could have spent the day at Dad's, you know. I'm sure eating in the Erik Burke shrine would have done wonders for your digestion."

"Your brother picked a fine time to remodel his kitchen."

"You know he's lying, right? The truth is, none of us can roast a turkey worth a damn and we eat here every Thanksgiving. It's kind of a family joke at this point. Whenever there's a family gathering, he claims he's having his kitchen remodeled. Except last year. Andie made Thanksgiving dinner for all of us, but they broke up shortly after that."

They checked their coats, and then he lifted her hand and kissed the stunning diamond ring she'd been sporting for several months before he laced their fingers together.

"What do you think the chances are the sweater makes it out alive?"

"We almost never throw food at each other." She grinned. "As a matter of fact, I think that was the very last Thanksgiving dinner we tried to make for ourselves. I like your family's Thanksgiving better."

It had been nothing short of a miracle that their schedules had lined up so they could eat dinner with Will's family. While Americans were celebrating Indigenous Peoples' Day in mid-October, Canadians were having Thanksgiving, and there had been enough of a gap in the hockey schedule and Kristen's work with a Boston nonprofit to allow for a rushed visit home.

The Lecroix family had welcomed Kristen with open arms, thrilled Will was happy and loved. The Burke family was...trying.

He squeezed her hand. "I think your father said about ten words to me at your birthday dinner. Let's see if we can get him up to a dozen today."

"My *no talking about hockey* rule is more at fault than any feelings he has about you. I mean, not that he's a fan, but it's more that he literally has nothing else to talk about."

"I feel like we could talk a little bit about hockey. In a general sense."

"Only if you want the general sense of hot turkey gravy in your lap."

He chuckled and kissed her forehead. "You're pretty cute for a jinx."

"Stop that."

When both the Marauders and the Harriers went out in the first round of the play-offs, stunned sports fans decided it had to be Kristen's fault. She'd jinxed them somehow by hooking up with her brother's rival. That had been fun.

Luckily, a series of bad calls decided the second round, and hockey fandom forgot about her as they united in turning on the refs.

So far this season, both teams were first place in their divisions, and the romance between Cross Lecroix and Erik Burke's sister was old news, so she was hopeful that episode wouldn't flare up again in the spring.

It was going to be a long time before Will let it go, though. He still thought it was hilarious, and she was going to have to update her will to add a clause forbidding him from adding it to her headstone.

Her father and brother were already at the table they'd reserved, and both of the Burke men stood when the host led Will and Kristen over. She hugged them each and then smiled when Will shook their hands without incident. The first time Lamont and Will had been introduced, her dad had tried to have one of those knuckle-crushing contests, and it was the last time he tried it with Will.

"So, the *Hometown Hoser* posted a video clip of you at last week's game," Erik said once they'd ordered a bottle of white wine and waters all around. The restaurant only offered turkey dinners on Thanksgiving, so they didn't have to order the food. "Joel had to point out you weren't wearing any team gear."

Kristen laughed, even though her brother had broken the no-hockey-talk rule within a minute of them sitting down. "It was the first time I gave in to watching you two play each other in person. It was harder than I thought it would be."

"Luckily, your brother never lets up on keeping his shoot-out skills sharp," Lamont said.

Will and Erik exchanged a look that wasn't quite a

mutual rolling of the eyes, and then Will said easily, "You win some, you lose some."

Lamont snorted, and Kristen felt the last of the anxiety she'd felt about this dinner fade away. Her dad was always going to take a shot on his son's behalf if he got the chance, but Will and Erik were okay. The years of professional animosity would always be there, but they were learning to leave it on the ice where it belonged. And for Kristen's sake, neither of them took Lamont's bait.

Despite the tentative peace, an awkward silence fell over the table until Lamont took a healthy swallow of wine and then cleared his throat. "So, Cross—uh, Will—Erik tells me you and your dad went on a fishing trip during the off-season. Have you done any deep-sea fishing when you're in Boston?"

"I've done a couple of excursions out of Baltimore, but never in Boston."

"Erik and I have talked about doing one next summer. You're welcome to join in if you want."

Will looked startled for a second, but he recovered quickly. "Sounds good. I'd be up for that."

As the servers set turkey dinners in front of them, Kristen leaned close to Will. "You should probably wear a life jacket."

He chuckled and squeezed her leg under the table before smothering everything on his plate in turkey gravy.

There was more hockey talk as they ate, but Kristen found she didn't mind. The men kept it civil, and she didn't feel that *nope* reflex in her gut that she used to. She even enjoyed going to the games, getting to know the wives and girlfriends of Will's teammates, and she'd even gone to a few of Erik's games. She divided her time between Boston and Baltimore since she could do most of her job remotely, but there were meetings and a few functions she needed to be in Boston for. The airport time could be a pain the ass, but they were making it work for the near future.

They hadn't told anybody yet, but Will had decided he'd play out the two years left in his contract and then hang up his skates so they could start a family. She was holding on to her apartment in Boston, but they had plenty of time to figure out where they wanted to go after Baltimore, and how they'd split their time between the US and Canada.

"Have you guys picked a date for the wedding yet?" Erik asked in a way that made it clear he was having a hard time coming up with conversation that wasn't about hockey.

"I was thinking we could squeeze it in during the All-Star break," she said, and then she laughed when all three men stopped eating to stare at her in horror. "I'm kidding. Next summer, at a resort near where Will's parents live."

Between her friends and Will's friends and teammates, they were pretty much renting the place out for a long weekend, but she knew it meant a lot to him to get married in Ontario.

"I never thought when I walked my daughter down the aisle and gave her away that I'd be giving her to Cross Lecroix," Lamont said, and Will's hand was on her leg again, gently squeezing. But her dad smiled and gave a quick disbelieving shake of his head before he went back to eating.

Later, after they'd consumed as much turkey and pie as they could eat and said goodbye to the Burke men, Will took her hand in his for the walk to her car.

"That went better than I expected," he said.

"He's trying," Kristen admitted. "I probably shouldn't tell him the accent colors at the wedding will be the Marauders colors."

He squeezed her hand. "How are you feeling about him walking you down the aisle?"

"I hadn't decided, but after tonight I'm willing to give him a chance. He's really making an effort. And if he starts being a jerk again, I'll put on the invitation that every guest has to wear a Marauders jersey."

He laughed as they reached the car, but instead of opening her door for her, he spun her around and backed her up against it. "Speaking of jerseys, what are my chances of seeing you wearing mine and nothing else tonight?"

She wrapped her arms around his neck, pulling him close. "I'll expect a hat trick out of you."

"I love when you talk hockey to me," he said before cupping the back of her neck and kissing her until the sounds of the city faded away. Then he ran his thumb over her bottom lip. "I love you."

"I love you, too." She smiled and cupped the side of his face. "I still can't believe I fell in love with a hockey player."

"Present tense."

"Yes, I *am* in love with a hockey player." She stood on her tiptoes for another kiss. "Forever."

A SECOND SHOT

1

———

Erik Burke navigated the streets leading out of Boston easily, one hand on the wheel as he sang along with the upbeat Christmas song blasting from the big luxury car's speakers. He couldn't sing worth a damn, but he didn't care. They'd won on the road against longtime rivals and now the Boston Marauders only had a couple of games at home and one short road trip before the Christmas break. The post-game media had stopped asking him about his sister falling for the opponent he'd dropped gloves with more times than he could count. Plus, they were in first place and he had the best left wing stats in their conference.

Throw in some holiday spirit and life was good. Sure, he was forcing the Christmas vibe a little. He was used to being alone, but this year he was even more lonely. But he wasn't going to sit in his house and feel sorry for himself. He was going to be jolly, dammit.

A furry shadow flashed in his headlights and he jammed on the breaks, swerving to avoid hitting whatever it was. Heart hammering in his chest, he pulled over and put the car in park. He looked in his rearview mirror, hoping he hadn't hit whatever it was. A raccoon, maybe.

It hadn't looked like a raccoon, though. It looked like a dog. And little dogs that could be mistaken for small raccoons shouldn't be out alone on a night like this.

"Shit." He hit the button to turn on his four-way flashers and got out of the car. Then he whistled the way he'd heard people who had dogs whistle for them.

He stayed next to his open door, though, just in case it wasn't a dog. But after a few seconds, he saw it coming toward him and it was definitely a dog. It was tiny and filthy and some of its fur was matted, but he was sure it was one of those breeds of dogs people usually pampered and bought fancy pillows for.

"What happened to you, little guy?" he asked as the dog got close enough for him to reach down and pick up. "Okay, so you're not a little guy, then."

She just whimpered as he cradled her in his arms, and licked his hand as she trembled hard enough to make the non-matted fur quiver.

He wasn't sure what to do with her at this point, but he knew she was cold and he could at least solve that problem for her. After sliding back into his car, he pulled the door shut with his free hand before turning on the seat heater for the passenger seat.

Then he reached into the back seat and unzipped his hockey bag. After rummaging for a second, he pulled out a sweatshirt. "Okay, dog, this may not smell good, but it's warm."

After making a nest for her in the passenger seat, he set the little dog down. She didn't seem to mind the smell. She pawed it at for a second and then turned around twice before nestling down in the soft fleece.

He rested his hand on her, feeling her tremble under his touch. "I think we need to have you checked out. You're just a little peanut and it looks like you've been out here for a while."

She lifted her head to lick his hand some more before burrowing into the sweatshirt and closing her eyes.

After using his phone to find the nearest animal hospital with an emergency room, he put on his seatbelt and put the car in gear. His passenger didn't seem to mind—or even notice—when it started to move, but he kept an eye on her in case she got scared.

When he parked near the entrance of the animal hospital and shut the car off, the dog lifted her head, but didn't look concerned. When he got out and closed his door, though, she sat up and watched him walk around the car with obvious anxiety. As he opened the passenger door, he could hear her crying, so he scooped her out of the sweatshirt and cuddled her against his chest.

The lights in the emergency clinic made him blink as he stepped up to the reception desk. There was a very young woman sitting behind it, and a woman he guessed was a vet by the white coat had her back to them, head bent as if she was reading something.

"Aw, poor baby." The receptionist's face softened as she looked at the dirty, shaking bundle of fur in his arms. "Somebody's had a rough go."

"I just finished up with a patient, so I'm available," the doctor said, turning.

Even before he saw her face, her voice knocked him on his ass. That voice used to brighten his days, but now he only heard it in dreams that left him feeling sad and lonely.

Andrea Morgan was his *one who got away* and losing her

was one of the very few regrets he had in his life. And by far the most painful.

"Andie," he said, voice cracking. "You told me you were moving."

It was a stupid thing to say but his mind seemed hung up on the fact she'd been in Boston the whole time.

"I was planning to, but then my sister told me she was pregnant and I didn't want to be that far away from her."

It was probably a good thing he had an armful of filthy, trembling dog because all he wanted to do was pull her into his arms, bury his hands in that mass of dark curls and kiss her until neither of them could breathe. But he'd lost the right to hold her a year ago when she asked for more from him and he couldn't give her what she'd needed.

God, he'd missed her.

When she spoke, her voice and the coolness in her dark eyes killed any hope of a warm reunion. "What are you doing here?"

He blinked, trying to kick his brain back into gear. "I need a vet."

"Do you know how many veterinary clinics there are in this city? What are you doing *here*?"

He realized she thought he'd chosen her specifically, so he shifted the dog in his arms so Andie could see her a little better. "I asked my phone for the nearest doggy emergency room and this was it."

Her attention shifted to the dog and his stomach tightened as her face softened. She loved animals and at least he knew that no matter how much she hated him, she would take care of his scared little hitchhiker.

～

THE CLINIC WAS the one place Andrea Morgan thought she'd be safe from running into Erik because he wasn't the kind of guy to get a pet.

Her day had been going pretty well, until six feet and two inches of blue-eyed hockey player walked through the doors. And he had the beard again, damn him. All scruffy and dark blond to match the thick hair she'd loved to run her fingers through.

Very aware that Jo was watching them as though they were a reality show filming in front of her desk, she tried her best to ignore the man as she looked over the pathetic looking dog shaking in his arms. It wasn't easy, since Erik had obviously showered recently and he smelled utterly distracting.

"I don't think she's hurt," he said in a soft voice. "Just cold and hungry, probably. She's been lost."

As much as she'd like to tell him to turn his ass around and get out of her life—again—she had a new little patient who needed her. "Bring her in here."

When she led him into a very small exam room, she cursed the lack of space they had. Not that the lobby of a grand hotel would be enough space to keep her body from being aware of his, but in here they'd practically be touching.

"Not very big for an animal hospital," he said with a chuckle.

She would have preferred to leave the door open, but for the animal's safety, it had to be closed before he could set the dog down. "I'm not sure what your phone told you, but we're a very small twenty-four-hour clinic. Animal hospital is quite the stretch."

"But you can take care of her?"

She pointed over her shoulder at her framed degrees

without looking away from the dog. "Put her down so I can take a look at her."

He did as he was told and then backed up as far as the tiny room allowed. Doing her best to block out his looming presence, she did a thorough examination of her patient. The dog wasn't hurt, as far as she could tell, and didn't appear to have been mistreated. She was dehydrated, of course, and the pads of her paws were pretty beat up.

"Her collar's gone, and she's not chipped," she said matter-of-factly when she was done with her exam.

"What does that mean?"

"It means we have no idea who she is or who she belongs to, and it'll take time to find out. Checking for lost dog reports and checking out the Facebook groups."

He frowned. "And in the meantime? What happens when somebody finds a dog and it's hurt and nobody knows who owns it?"

"She'll stay in the kennel until she recovers and, if we still haven't located her owner, we'll try to find a foster home for her or a shelter. She might have been abandoned, in which case there's nobody out there to claim her."

"But you'll still take care of her?"

"I'm not tossing her back out on the street, Erik. Sometimes the clinic can donate care and there are crowdfunding options. Once the dog's recovered, it can be sent to a shelter, but dogs with medical issues are..." She let the thought die away and shook her head. "If the injuries are more severe and it looks like the animal will need care beyond what shelters or a foster family can provide, it's often more humane to let them go."

He stared at the dog for a long moment and she watched his throat work as he swallowed hard before giving her a tight smile. "That's very sad. It's a good thing Peanut isn't a stray, I guess. Right, Peanut?"

The dog, reacting to the change in his voice as he spoke to her, looked up at him adoringly and licked his hand.

Andie wasn't sure what to make of this Erik—the version of him that cared about anything but hockey. Peanut wasn't his dog. She'd bet money Peanut wasn't even the dog's name. He'd found a dog injured on the side of the road or something and he couldn't bring himself to abandon it.

But, even though it had been a year since she saw him, she'd gotten to know him well enough to see the glimmer of panic in his eyes. He might not want to drop Peanut with her and run, but he also didn't know the first thing about taking care of a dog. He'd never wanted a pet because of his schedule. Hell, he hadn't even been able to make room for a woman, never mind a dog.

Despite getting a perverse satisfaction out of watching him squirm, there was Peanut to consider, so she offered Erik an out. "Sometimes we can find a donor who's willing to fund the animal's medical expenses, even after they go into a foster home. Or even their forever home. It's easier to place a pet with medical needs if the family doesn't have to take on the financial burden."

He sighed, watching the dog lick the back of his hand. Andie knew he was considering her words because he always got worry lines between his brows when he was deep in thought. But then Peanut tried to burrow under his big hand, as if to find shelter there.

Andie didn't blame the dog. She knew all too well how much comfort those hands could offer. And how much... She cleared her throat and it sounded harsh in the quiet room.

Erik let out a long sigh. "I should have my business

manager look into helping fund stuff like that. Right, little Peanut?"

"I'd like to keep her overnight. They can keep an eye on her, get her cleaned up and do some blood work. You can come back in the morning."

He'd push back now, she thought. It was one thing to invest time and energy into a dog during the evening hours. But not if his so-called Peanut was going to start messing up his daily schedule.

And he did hesitate for a long moment. Here it comes, she thought. The truth would come out because it was more convenient for him. But then he nodded. "Okay. Will you be here in the morning?"

She was so surprised he hadn't balked at giving the dog more of his time, she didn't have time to emotionally brace herself when Erik turned all of his attention back to her. "I… Yes. I'll be here tomorrow."

"Good."

Had his eyes always been that intense shade of blue? She knew they had, but for some reason they seemed extra potent today. "I have stuff to do, so say goodbye and then you can stop at the desk on your way out. They'll need all of your information to go with Peanut's records. And for billing, of course."

"Be a good girl, Peanut, and get stronger," he said, stroking the dog's head. She thought he'd walk out then, but he remained silent until she looked up at him again. "I'll see you tomorrow."

After he'd gone out the door and closed it behind him, Andie looked at the little dog. "Look what you did, Peanut."

The dog just rested her chin on her paws and watched her. With a sigh, Andie picked her up and went out the back door of the exam room to the hallway that ran to the kennel area so she could find Peanut a warm bed. And they needed to get her cleaned up and push some fluids into her.

Chelsea, the other vet who worked during the day, practically fell through the open door of the exam room when she went back to clean it up for the next patient. "Tell me that wasn't Erik Burke."

"Okay, it wasn't Erik Burke."

Chelsea's eyes narrowed. "You're lying."

"I'm not lying. Just doing what I'm told."

"Andie! *Was* that freaking Erik Burke or not?"

"Yes, it was freaking Erik Burke." She pointed her finger at Chelsea. "You are not allowed to make a big deal out of him being here."

"I have a signed picture of him hoisting the Cup hanging on my living room wall, Andie. It's a very big deal."

Andie wasn't big on personal sharing in the work place. In her experience, it led to drama and gossip and she preferred to keep her focus on their patients. And if she told Chelsea the truth about her history with Erik, it wouldn't be kept quiet. Everybody in the clinic—and possibly everybody knew Chelsea had ever met or friended on Facebook— would know Andie had dated the city's favorite left winger.

"The animals are our patients, but their owners' information is confidential," she reminded Chelsea. "And he's coming back in the morning for Peanut. Don't make a fuss or he'll be uncomfortable."

That was a lie. The Erik she knew had loved having a fuss made over him when it came to hockey. When it came to all things off the ice, he wasn't as good with other people's emotions, though.

"I'm a professional," Chelsea insisted, though the excited gleam in her eye made Andie nervous.

As if she didn't have enough to be anxious about. She

didn't have the mental bandwidth to worry about how Chelsea would react to Erik walking through the doors tomorrow morning.

She had enough to worry about when it came to herself. She had a little more than twelve hours, give or take a few, to get a hold of herself before she saw him again.

Forget the blue eyes, she told herself. Forget how just the sight of him made her pulse quicken. She needed to remember how much it had hurt when he'd let her walk out his door for the last time.

She couldn't let herself forget that when it came to a choice between hockey and Andie, Erik chose the game every time.

2

Erik tossed his bag on the floor and his keys on the table, kicking the door closed behind him. Usually his mind would be turning the game over and over in a constant replay loop. Analyzing his play. Noting his mistakes. Cataloging his aches and pains, though they didn't matter. Mentally telling himself what he needed to do better for the next game.

Tonight there was only one thing on his mind.

Andie.

Taking Peanut into the clinic and coming face to face with Andrea Morgan had blown every other thought out of his head.

Walking away from her was the stupidest move he'd ever made. They'd been together eight months and they'd been the best eight months of his life, but like every relationship he'd ever had with a woman, it started taking time and focus away from his game.

His phone rang and the few seconds he thought it might be Andie were a rollercoaster. There was the spike in his pulse at the thought of talking to her again, but then he was afraid she might be calling with bad news about Peanut.

But it was his sister, Kristen, and he flopped down on the couch as he answered. "Hey, Kris."

"Are you home?"

"Literally just walked in the door."

"Good game," she said, and he knew that she meant it, but she also didn't call to talk about it. That would be his dad's call once he let him know he was home. While falling in love with a hockey player had loosened her up a bit, to say she wasn't a hockey fan was an understatement. Before she hooked up with Cross, she'd actually hated the game, probably because of all the sacrifices the family had made for Erik's career.

"Thanks," he said. "What's up?"

"Are you going to Dad's for Christmas break?"

It seemed like an odd question. "I'd planned on it. Why?"

"Is he going to be a dick if I bring Will over?"

Lamont Burke wasn't any more of a fan of Will "Cross" Lecroix than Erik had been, but the guy wasn't actually that bad. And he was head-over-heels for Kristen. They were happy, so Erik was willing to leave their rivalry on the ice. "I'll talk to him. I think he'll be okay, though. He's getting used to the idea and now when Cross comes up, most of the words that come out of his mouth could be said on TV."

"Network or cable?"

Erik chuckled. "Give him time. Oh hey, I got a dog."

There was a long silence. "What do you mean, you got a dog?"

"I found her and now I have a dog."

"Erik, you need to back up." He could tell she'd put him

on speakerphone, but she only did that when she was alone. "You found her?"

"She ran across the road in front of me and I stopped. She's spending the night at the clinic because she's obviously been on her own for a while. But she's cute and she likes me."

"Last time I suggested you get a dog or a cat or a damn fish or anything to keep you company, you said you couldn't care for a pet because you spend too much time on the road."

"Yes, I did say that. And it's still true, but you can help us out with that, right Auntie Kristen?"

"Don't call me that, and I am not babysitting your dog, Erik."

"But she's—"

"No. Nope. Not a chance."

"You should meet her," he said. "She's the cutest little thing."

"There are plenty of kids out there who'd love to babysit the cutest little thing."

Erik frowned. "You want me to leave her with some random kid I find on the internet?"

"You found her on the side of the road." Erik was very offended on Peanut's behalf, so he didn't respond. Kristen finally broke the awkward silence with a sigh. "Okay. I'll help you, but I'm not going to be your dog sitter. I'm busy. But I'll help you find somebody who will take really good care of Peanut because she's had a rough go and she deserves to be a princess."

"Thank you," he said, relieved she was on board. He knew she'd give in because she loved animals and she had a hard time resisting her brother, too, but she had a lot going on in her own life.

"I'll get back to you tomorrow sometime with some potentials."

"Thanks." And then, because it was on his mind and he needed to talk about it, he spilled the rest. "So there's more to the story."

"There's *more*? I'm still trying to get over picturing you with a dog."

"The vet I took her to was...somebody from my past."

"Yeah, you're going to have to narrow that down. *Way* down."

He rolled his eyes, even though she couldn't see him. "Andrea Morgan."

Kristen sucked in an audible breath. "Oh, shit."

Those two words meant Kristen got it and he wouldn't have to explain why it was a big deal. She could probably guess how rocked he was by seeing Andie again, which was good since he didn't really want to vocalize it.

"That was the first time you've seen her since the break-up, right?" she asked.

"Yeah." When he was awake, anyway. He dreamed about her a lot.

"That must have been quite the emotional sucker-punch." That was his sister, always getting right to the heart of a thing. "How was she?"

"She didn't throw anything at me or try to stab me with a doggy needle or anything, but I wouldn't say she was happy to see me."

"I wouldn't expect her to be. Not after...what happened."

What happened. Such a bland way of describing the day he'd broken Andie's heart and probably ruined any chance of happiness he'd ever have, not that he'd realized that at the time. At the time, he'd been almost proud of himself—proud of his laser focus on his game, because hockey was the only thing that mattered. It was how his father had raised him. Hockey first. He'd never amount to much if he let anything affect his game.

"She's going to be there tomorrow when I pick up Peanut," he said.

"I still can't believe you have a dog."

He couldn't believe it, either. He still wasn't sure what he was going to do with her, but he sure as hell couldn't just dump her with a vet—even if it was Andie—and walk away. "What should I say to her?"

"Sit. Stay. No, you can't have my bacon."

"I mean Andie, smartass." He snorted. "And she can have my bacon."

"If that's meant as some kind of sexual euphemism, I'm hanging up on you."

"No, I mean I would literally share my bacon with her."

"So let me get this straight," Kristen said in a tone that made Erik wince because he wasn't going to like whatever she was about to say next. "You wouldn't make room in your twenty-four-seven living and breathing hockey life, but you'll share your bacon with her? I'm just trying to nail down your rating system."

"That's harsh, Kris." Her words—deserved though they may be—cut him like a blade. "And you're not exactly unbiased since you hate hockey."

She sighed. "I hated that hockey devoured our lives and didn't leave much room for me, so yeah, I'm not unbiased when it comes to Andie feeling like she wasn't as important to you as the game and being hurt by it."

"And yet you still hooked up with a hockey player."

"If by *hooked up*, you mean I'm marrying one, yeah. But Will is...it's just different. And he loves me more than he loves the game."

Erik sucked on the inside of his cheek for a few seconds, keeping his mouth shut to keep himself from saying something stupid. He was happy for his sister, but it still smarted a little that she'd found her Prince Charming in Cross Lecroix—the Lex Luthor to Erik's Superman. Or maybe Erik was Lex Luthor. Either way, they weren't friends.

They were learning to be, though, because when they took off their skates, the one thing they had in common—loving Kristen—was more powerful than a career-long rivalry.

"You're deflecting the conversation back to me," Kristen said after a long silence. "Because you don't want to talk about you and Andie. What are you doing, Erik?"

"I don't know." It was the truth.

"Don't play with her. Assuming she's even willing to open that door again, you know the price of admission. Don't knock if you're not willing to pay."

"I'm not ready to retire." It was around the corner, like catching glimpses of the shadow of a creature waiting to jump out and scare him, but he wasn't there yet.

"The fact you still think that's what she was asking of you is why nothing has changed." Another dramatic sigh. "It's not an all-or-nothing thing, and until you figure that out, you need to leave her alone."

"I can't leave her alone. She has my dog."

"I'm hanging up now. I'll ask around tomorrow and try to come up with some potential names to help you out."

"Thanks. Goodnight, Kristen."

He tossed his cell on the cushion next to him and rested his head against the buttery soft leather.

The fact you still think that's what she was asking of you is why nothing has changed.

What had changed was that, for the first time in his life,

there was a hole that hockey didn't fill. But maybe with a little Christmas luck and with the help of a little lost dog, he'd get a second chance.

~

AFTER A RESTLESS NIGHT spent trying to remember the bad times instead of the good times when it came to Erik, Andie decided she'd need an extra-large coffee to get through the morning. And as she waited in line at her favorite coffee shop, she thought about how poorly she'd done at achieving that objective.

She'd carried the lingering pain of their breakup with her for the last year, but last night she'd only been able to remember the way his eyes crinkled when he laughed and the delicious smell of him when he was freshly showered. And, lord help her, she had *no* trouble remembering how good the man had been in bed. The first time they'd gotten naked together, his big and very muscled frame had made her nervous, but his touch was the perfect blend of gentleness and strength.

She'd missed that touch. A lot.

"Your regular, Andie?"

She blinked, realizing she'd gotten to the front of the line. "Extra-large this morning, please. And, what the hell, throw in a raspberry danish, too."

Sugar with her extra caffeine was probably a mistake, but she was going to be seeing Erik again very soon, and she needed the boost. She suspected that, even if she found something to keep her occupied in the exam rooms or lab, he would wait. Seeing Peanut wouldn't be enough. The intensity in his gaze when he left last night made it clear he wouldn't leave without seeing her, as well.

After greeting the other staff members, Andie locked herself in her tiny office and turned her computer on to review the notes from the overnight staff. It had been a quiet night, she thought as she ate the pastry over a napkin to keep sticky crumbs from falling into her keyboard. They couldn't afford to replace any equipment right now.

Pulling up Peanut's file, she skimmed the notes and the lab results. If there was cause for concern, they had to send samples out to a lab because they didn't have the equipment or staff for in-depth analysis, but Peanut was in the clear. She was surprisingly healthy for a dog who'd obviously been on her own for a while in cold temperatures, and she'd be able to go home today.

Home with Erik, she thought, and the corners of her mouth quirked into a smile.

He was going to have to put up or shut up today. It was one thing to claim Peanut when she'd be in the care of the clinic overnight. It was entirely another when he was going to have a dog in his house. A dog who not only required a laundry list of items, but his affection and attention.

Erik was good at providing things. He wasn't careless with his money, but he was generous. And he was even good at giving affection. But he fell down when it came to attention. Only one thing ever got his full attention and that was hockey.

This time a year ago, she'd been struggling to find her place in Erik's life. She knew he loved her, but their time together came after everything else. Not only practices and games, though. And not even time with the trainers and watching games and meetings. Even listening to his dad rehash every mistake he'd made in a game came before giving Andie his attention. When she'd told him it was time to go home with her for Christmas and not only meet her family, but spend three hockey-free days together during the league break, he'd balked. When she'd pushed, he'd shut the idea down and she'd walked out his door for the last time.

By the time Erik arrived, Andie was as ready as she could be to face him again. He wouldn't have the element of surprise this time, and she'd wrapped memories of their parting around her like armor.

She even managed to sound professional when he looked at her with those blue eyes and said her name in a husky voice that made her shiver. "Andie. How did you sleep?"

"Fine, thank you." Chelsea was staring at them, so Andie was relieved when the vet tech walked through the kennel doors holding Peanut.

"Look at her!" Erik grinned and reached out for the little dog who was squirming with eagerness to get to him. "You're a pretty little girl, aren't you?"

She was, Andie thought. Mostly white, with a little tan in her fluffy hair. Probably a mixed breed, but a cute one. Andie didn't miss his surprise at how pretty Peanut was, which was only natural since he'd never seen the dog clean.

"Is she okay? Ready to go home?" he asked, obviously intending to keep up the pretense.

"Let's step into a room." Being closed up in a small space with him again probably wasn't her best idea, but she also didn't want to conduct their business with Chelsea watching.

Once she'd closed the door, she practically had to flatten herself against the wall to get around him without their bodies actually touching. "Set her down on the table and we can go over her paperwork."

"She's okay, right?"

The pang of nervousness in his voice turned her insides to mush. *No*, she told herself. No mush around this man. "She's healthy. A little underweight and she was dehydrated, but that's to be expected since, well, I'm sure you know exactly how long she's been lost."

He didn't answer, pretending to be too busy fussing over the dog. The effect watching those big hands scratching behind tiny ears had on Andie was ridiculous and she cleared her throat. It sounded loud and harsh in the small room, and it made him look up at her.

"Even though you obviously don't need it, since Peanut is your dog," she said, handing him a sheet of paper and trying not to smile. "It's standard procedure to give this list to every dog owner when we discharge a patient for the first time. It covers basic care and necessities."

The list being standard procedure was a lie, but she wanted to watch his face when he looked at it. And he didn't disappoint as he skimmed the list. His expression went from casual interest to furrowed concentration to an incredulous *you have got to be kidding me* as he read. It was an exhaustive list, to be sure.

He sighed and held up the list for Peanut to see. "Really?"

Andie had to choke down her laughter when the dog yipped and sat up on her haunches so her tongue could reach his hand. She licked him once and then gazed adoringly at him.

"We do have some collars and leashes for sale from a local company out front," she said. "Since you didn't bring Peanut's with you today."

"Oh...yeah." He stroked the dog's back a couple of times and then shoved his hands in his pockets. "I didn't think of it. I'll buy some before we leave."

As much as Andie had enjoyed the game of making Erik uncomfortable, she couldn't in good conscience allow him to take Peanut home with him. He was obviously unprepared and if he got overwhelmed—or Peanut interfered with his hockey—she didn't want him surrendering her to just any shelter. She'd rather handle that herself.

"Look, Erik," she said, trying to inject some authority into her voice. "We both know Peanut isn't your dog. While she clearly fell madly in love with you at first sight, she was also alone and cold and scared. If we can't find her real owner, we'll make sure she finds somebody new to fall in love with."

Frowning, he picked Peanut up. She looked tiny in his strong arms, and Andie's heart melted a little when Peanut rubbed the top of her head against Erik's beard and he smiled. "She loves me."

"Trust me, she'll get over you."

She flung the bitter words at him without thinking and watched them land. His smile faded and the fingers idly scratching under Peanut's chin stilled. He was silent, looking at her with those deep blue eyes that gave nothing away.

"She can stay with me while you look for her owner," he said finally, but some of the light had gone out of his eyes. "I can't handle the idea of her being alone in a cage, even if she has all the material things she needs. Please, Andie. Just let her go home with me and if we find her owner, then I'll bring her back."

She shouldn't, but both the man and the dog stared at her with pleading eyes before Peanut buried her head under Erik's hand.

"Erik."

"I won't let her down. I promise."

There was something in the way he said the words that

broke Andie's resolve. Taking care of this little dog was important to him and maybe he was even trying to prove something to himself.

"On one condition." She pointed her finger at him. "If you decide she's too much or you can't take care of her, you call me. Do *not* bring her to whatever shelter your phone tells you is the closest."

"I promise." He grinned. "I'll call you."

And he did, hours later and just as she was getting ready to leave the clinic. But he wasn't trying to offload Peanut. He was trying to shop for her.

"I looked online, but there's so much, Andie. And I don't know what sizes and what's safe and...I need your help. Please go shopping with me, and then I won't ask you for anything else."

Why did she have such a hard time saying no to this man?

3

"She probably doesn't even like hockey."

Erik crossed his arms and looked at the pile he'd just deposited in his shopping cart. Okay, maybe it was a bit much, but Andie didn't know Peanut any better than she did. "She's Erik Burke's dog, so of course she likes hockey."

"If you start referring to yourself in the third person, I'm walking out right now."

He laughed, even though he knew she was serious. Then he held up the little doggie dress with the Marauders logo emblazoned on it in rhinestones. "Do you think this will fit her?"

"*That* is ridiculous."

"You're the one who brought me to a pet store with Marauders gear. I had no idea they made so much hockey stuff for dogs."

"First, the hockey stuff is for the owners, not the dogs. Second, you didn't know that because you don't actually *have* a dog. And third, I'm a little concerned about her swallowing any of that bling."

He scowled at the dozens of tiny pieces of plastic and put it back. "What about one of these purse things?"

The idea of Erik carrying Peanut around in a purse made her laugh out loud. He frowned, obviously confused, and she laughed even harder.

"Don't dogs like Peanut like being carried around in bags?"

Somehow she managed to get herself under control. "The only bag you carry is a hockey bag and as a veterinarian, I can tell you the stench would make her very ill."

"She liked my sweatshirt when I put it on the seat for her to curl up on last night."

"She was hungry, cold and alone, but I bet she still thought twice before touching it."

He laughed as they moved on down the aisle, without the dog purse. He'd always loved her laugh. Her looks and the way she carried herself had caught his attention at the small deli he liked to frequent on his very infrequent cheat days, but it was her laugh that had made him approach her. Being with her felt so right—so normal—that he could almost forget they'd spent the last year apart.

Almost.

"What are you planning to do with Peanut when you're not home?" She asked when they hit an aisle that looked dedicated to keeping animals contained in yards. Then she turned her head to look at him, her dark gaze locking with his. "Actually, where is she right now?"

"If I'd known she was allowed in this store, I would have brought her. Right now she's closed in my bedroom." When her eyebrow arched, he shrugged. "I know, it's not perfect, but I wasn't sure what else to do. I took her out, and then I put food and water down for her. I closed the door to the bathroom because I don't *think* she's big enough to get up on the toilet, but I didn't want her to fall in. And I don't have a bed for her yet, so I dragged my comforter onto the floor and made her a nest. I thought, because it smells like me, she'd probably be okay until I get home."

Her expression was so soft and inviting when he finished speaking, he almost leaned down and kissed her. But then her lips tightened and she shook her head. "Damn you, Erik Burke."

"Shit. You don't think she'll get wrapped up in the blanket, do you? She's so tiny and—"

"It's not the dog, Erik," she snapped, and then she started walking fast, past things he was pretty sure were on the list she'd given him.

"Andie, wait." He caught her elbow and spun her around to face him. "What just happened?"

"What happened is that you're being so sweet and adorable and it makes me forget you're not capable of letting anybody into your life." She snorted. "A dog, I guess. For now. But not a woman who loved you."

As stupid as it was, since they'd been broken up for a year, hearing her say she'd loved him in the past tense hurt more than the nasty check from Lecroix in the last game of the season two years before. "I'm sorry I'm being adorable."

He watched the battle on her face and then rejoiced when whatever part of her trying to resist him lost the fight and she laughed. "You should be."

"It just comes naturally to hockey players. We can't help it."

She rolled her eyes and waved a hand at all the things she'd just speed-walked past. "Do you need yard stuff for her?"

"I don't think so. She doesn't go outside unattended at all and never goes more than a few feet from me. And the girl who's probably going to be stopping in to take her out and visit with her when I'm not home isn't going to just stick her outside, either."

By the time they'd gone up and down the aisles, buying everything Peanut needed as well as a few really cute things she didn't, Erik was starving. It was well past dinner time and he needed to eat.

He thought about it while Andie helped him load his purchases into his car. She needed to eat, too. And she'd done him a huge favor. Even without the way her body stretched as she reached into his trunk and the ache of his body remembering how good hers felt under him, it would be rude not to offer to feed her.

"Where do you want to eat?" he asked, and then inwardly winced at the lack of smoothness in his game at the moment.

"What?" She actually looked startled by the question.

"I'm starving. And you have to let me buy you dinner after all this."

He hated watching her emotions play over her face, but he forced himself to be quiet and wait. If she didn't want to have dinner with him, he'd have to accept that, but he wasn't ready to say goodbye to her yet. "Just as a thank you. Please, Andie."

ANDIE SHOULD RUN. She should turn around and run to her car, drive home and then eat a gallon of ice cream while forcing herself to relive every painful detail of their breakup. And then she should make a note in Peanut's file that she was Chelsea's patient exclusively and never, ever see Erik again. In less than twenty-four hours, he'd turned her life upside down again and if she had dinner with him, it was only going to get worse.

Her head was telling her no was definitely the right move. But her heart—and points south—wanted more Erik. And then her traitorous stomach, neglected since the danish that morning, growled and she knew she was sunk.

"I could eat," she admitted, since the twitch at the corners of his mouth let her know her hunger hadn't gone unnoticed. "No place fancy, though. You don't need to show off for me. I just want food."

"I don't show off," he grumbled.

She nodded her head toward the very expensive car attached to the door he held open for her to make her point, but then didn't get in. "I should just follow you wherever we're going."

He hesitated for a few seconds before closing the door. "There's a place up the street that's got great pasta. We could walk there."

She knew it was his way of respecting her wishes not to ride together while also not taking separate vehicles, but she also knew the restaurant he was talking about and it did have damn good pasta. "Sounds good."

By the time her fettuccine carbonara arrived, the sensation of having stumbled into a weird time warp had set in. The Erik sitting across the table from her was the Erik she'd fallen in love with. He was funny and charming and so attentive to her, she felt as if they were the only two people in the world.

Mostly he asked her about the clinic, since that had come about after their break-up. She didn't necessarily want to talk about her work, but she definitely didn't want to talk about *his* work, since it was hard to bring him back once his brain latched onto hockey talk. And she didn't want to rehash the end of their relationship, so the clinic was the best bet.

And because she knew him so well, she saw the signals. The way the corners of his mouth turned up a little whenever their eyes met. The way his leg rested against hers under the table as if it was simply a lack of space because he was so damn tall. His fingertips tracing circles in the condensation on his water glass. His focus was on her, but there was a part of him already wondering how soon they could fall into bed.

When they'd walked slowly back to where they were parked, she was ready when he made his move.

"It's going to take me forever to get all that dog stuff in the house," he said after clearing his throat. The fact he was nervous made him extra adorable, she thought. "Can I talk you into following me home and helping me out? I mean, I don't want Peanut getting out while I'm making all those trips."

She laughed at his attempt to use his dog to soften her up. He didn't need to because she'd made up her mind before he even paid the bill that she'd go home with him if he asked her. She hadn't been with anybody since leaving Erik and if she went home without scratching that itch, she was going to toss and turn every night for weeks.

"I'd hate for Peanut to get lost again," she said, rolling with his flimsy excuse.

Even though Andie knew how to get to his house, she appreciated that he drove a little slower than he usually did so he didn't lose her. Those were the kind of actions that had drawn her in the first time, showing her what a sweet and considerate man he was under all that hockey player. And he waited for her in the driveway so they could walk to the door together.

"You know your way around," he said as he opened it. "Make yourself at home while I check on Peanut and see if she destroyed my bedroom while I was gone. Then maybe you can watch her while I carry stuff in."

"Sure." It was hard, being back in the house that had been like a second home to her during the last few months of their relationship. Her apartment was on the small side and didn't have the big leather furniture or king-sized bed he liked, so they'd spent most of their time at his place. They'd been teetering on the brink of the *moving in* conversation—or maybe even a ring—when she'd had enough of trying to fit into his life.

"She was still curled up on my comforter," he said when he'd reappeared with Peanut in his arms. "I don't think she even moved."

"I'll take her out for a walk while you carry the stuff in."

By the time he was finished bringing in the haul, Andie and Peanut were curled up on the couch and they watched him struggle to put together a wire kennel. Once he was done, he fitted it with the little bed that had a very big price tag, along with a Marauders blanket.

Then he grinned at the dog. "Hey, Peanut. Isn't this nice?"

She hopped down and went to him, but she was a lot more interested in Erik holding her than she was the over-priced doggy bedroom.

"You know she's going to sleep with you," Andie said dryly.

"Yeah, but..." He stood and put his hands on his hips, staring down at Peanut with an expression that might have frightened a dog who didn't already know he was a sap.

"But what?" Andie shrugged. "She'll get used to it and she'll feel cozy in there while nobody's home. Trust me."

"That's not..." He laughed and ran a hand through his hair. "I'm not really worried about that."

Andie laughed so abruptly she startled Peanut. "You don't know what to do with her when you want to have sex."

"It's not funny."

"It is, a little."

He gave her the same scowl he'd given the dog. "This is a real problem."

"No, it's not. Put her in there, give her a pat and tell her goodnight. Or that you'll be back later."

"I'll worry she's lonely. Or crying."

"If you're worried your spoiled dog is crying in her luxury memory foam bed, you're not doing sex right."

His eyebrow arched as he gave her a wicked grin. "Is that a challenge?"

Ten minutes later, Andie was naked in Erik's bed and she was fairly confident the dog was the farthest thing from his mind.

"I've missed you," he growled against her bare breast, and she squirmed because the vibration tickled. "And I should warn you, nobody's going to write songs about tonight because it's been a freaking year and I have as much self-control as a teenager right now."

His words answered a question she hadn't dared ask—even in her own mind—and she ran her fingernails up his back. "I've missed you, too. And this."

Erik did his best, she had to admit. He stroked every part of her. Tasted. He kissed her so thoroughly she forgot everything except his mouth on hers. And when he finally took her, his gaze locked with hers and all the emotions they weren't expressing were there for her to see.

I love you. It was in his eyes. In his touch. In the way he made sure every stroke pleased her. And she wanted him to say it—wanted to say the words to him—but she closed her eyes and focused on the sensations as they both found a much-needed release.

When he'd disposed of the condom and hauled her into his arms, she scratched her fingernails lazily over his chest. He'd never been much of a talker after sex, but the way he held her and kissed her hair made her smile.

But as his breathing slowed and his muscles started relaxing, Andie knew it was time to go. She didn't want to spend the night because it would be awkward in the morning. They hadn't talked about their relationship—past or present—and she didn't know what this meant. They'd missed the sex. They'd missed each other's company. But coming together again didn't magically solve the issues that had driven them apart in the first place.

When she pulled away, he stirred. "You should stay."

"I have to be at work early tomorrow." She dropped a kiss on his shoulder before sliding out of bed. "I'll take Peanut out before I go and then put her back in her kennel."

He made a sleepy sound. "I think she wants to sleep with me. Just let her back in and she'll find me."

But she knew that once Erik fell asleep, he slept hard and Peanut couldn't jump that high, so after taking her outside, Andie carried the little dog into the bedroom and set her on the bed. Peanut immediately went and nestled against Erik's side, and Andie smiled and scratched her ears before dropping a kiss on Erik's mouth and leaving.

She was in so much trouble.

4

"Tell me everything." Chelsea leaned against the door jamb of Andie's tiny office, holding her coffee mug. "And the first patient's due in five minutes, so talk fast."

"Tell you what?"

"Tell me about the giant bouquet of flowers on the reception desk addressed to you, from Erik Burke."

Andie didn't really want to talk about it yet, if ever. Her body was still sore in all the best ways, but her heart was sore, too. Sleeping with Erik again was definitely a mistake. But it was a delicious mistake she was having trouble regretting.

"We've gotten flowers from clients before," she hedged.

"Not flowers like that. And I saw the smile when you read the card. That was an *I had great sex* smile." She glanced at the clock on the wall. "Talk faster."

"Fine, but if it leaves this room, I'll never trust you again." When Chelsea crossed her heart, Andie sighed and then told her a very abridged version of the Erik Burke story.

"Holy crap," Chelsea whispered when she was done. "I can't believe you almost moved into his house. Is it nice? I bet it's nice."

"Since we have about forty-five seconds left, maybe focus less on his decor and more on the fact he broke my heart and yet I appear to be going back for more."

"Okay, I'm going to put the whole hockey thing in a box...for now." Chelsea gave her a warm smile. "Are you going back for more because the sex is great and why not? Or are you going back for more because you're not over him and maybe you still love him?"

"I'm not over him. And I still love him. I don't see myself ever *not* loving him." Andie paused. "But also, the sex *is* great."

"I'm going to walk away now because I have a picture of the man on my wall. I wear his jersey. There's no way this doesn't get weird." Chelsea straightened. "Also, I hate you a little bit right now."

Andie laughed as her friend walked away, not taking it personally. She'd had sex with a man half the women in Boston lusted after, so it was to be expected. But she was sure they didn't fantasize about the reality of loving a professional athlete. It wasn't all fast cars and orgasms.

"Speak of the naughty devil," she muttered to herself when her cell phone rang and his number showed on the screen. "Hello?"

"Are you busy?"

"I have a few minutes. Mrs. Coleman's always late because she always thinks this is the day her cat won't hide and will go straight into the carrier without a fight. What's up?"

"I got a little distracted last night and forgot, but I need to ask a huge favor of you. I wouldn't, but I don't have anybody else to ask except Kristen and she won't do it."

"Do what?" His own sister not doing whatever it was for him sounded ominous.

"I've got a road game—just an overnight—and I just found out the girl Kristen found to dog sit for me doesn't do sleepovers. Is there any chance you can take Peanut for me? She really likes you."

And that was one of the reasons Erik had never considered a pet. An overnight trip wasn't a big deal, but what about when he played on the west coast and was gone a week? It happened too often during the season for a kennel to be a good option.

"I think Peanut really likes everybody," she said, trying to buy herself a little more time to think. Being sucked back into Erik's life probably wasn't great for her emotional health, but saying no to him wasn't easy. Add one adorable stray dog and it was damn near impossible. "But you can drop her off here and she can hang out, and then I'll take her home with me."

"You don't want to stay at my place?"

It would probably be easier. All of Peanut's many belongings were there. But she didn't want to slide back into the same relationship they'd had before. It would be so easy, until it wasn't.

"I'll take her to my place," she said, firmly. But then she gave just a little. "But I'll bring her home before you get there and wait for you."

"Something to look forward to," he said in a husky voice that left no doubt what exactly he was looking forward to.

Andie was busy when Erik dropped Peanut off, helping Chelsea with a dog who decided a glass Christmas tree ornament would be a good snack, so she didn't get a kiss goodbye. Just a text message telling her he couldn't wait for her but he'd call her later and see her the next day.

When she was finally free for a few minutes, she got Peanut out of the kennel and took her for a short walk. The little dog was thrilled to see her, but Andie happened to be looking at her when Peanut heard a group of little girls laughing. After a second, the dog appeared to sigh and then kept walking, but with a little less pep in her step.

She needed to dig a little deeper into lost dog reports, Andie thought. Maybe look statewide or beyond, and reach out to some people who might be able to help her. If Peanut had a family looking for her, the sooner they were reunited, the better. For Peanut *and* for Erik. He was getting attached to the tiny dog.

And she'd do well not to get too attached, either, she reminded herself. To the dog *or* the man.

ERIK PULLED into his driveway in probably the best mood he'd ever been in after a rough loss. His body ached and the post-game media questions had been brutal, but Andie's car in front of his garage, which meant she and Peanut were waiting inside for him.

As soon as he opened the door, he heard the clicking of Peanut's nails as she ran across the polished hardwood and the sound made him grin in anticipation. He knelt down to scoop her into his arms and accept the frantic licking she welcomed him home with. Then he carried her through the ground floor, looking for Andie.

He found her in the small sitting room at the back of the

house. It wasn't a room he spent a lot of time in, but she'd always liked it. Small and cozy, with furniture more about comfort than looks and big windows, she'd loved to curl up with a book when he was busy.

"Welcome home," she said, setting the book she'd been reading on the side table.

The words, simple as they were, warmed his soul. He could easily get used to this. Sitting in the loveseat that faced her chair, he settled Peanut on his lap, expecting her to curl up and fall asleep. Instead, she sat on his thigh and gazed up at him adoringly.

Yeah, he could *definitely* get used to this.

"It's good to be home." He could see the indecision on her face—to bring up the game or not to bring up the game —so he nodded toward the empty cushion next to him. "It would be better if you were sitting over here with me, though."

Andie uncurled her legs and stood, and they both chuckled when Peanut's tail wagged in anticipation. And when Andie was settled against him, stroking the dog while she leaned her head against his shoulder, Erik would swear his heart sighed. It was corny, he thought, but that's what it felt like.

He picked up the remote and started flipping through the channels. There was a west coast game on and he paused, knowing if he was alone, he'd toss the remote down and watch it. But then he kept surfing until he found repeats of an old sit-com they both liked.

"Did you have any problems with her while I was gone?" he asked, stroking Peanut's ear.

"None at all. She spent the day at the clinic being utterly spoiled by the entire staff. Then she went home with me and we watched a movie before she curled up in my bed. I'm still not sure how such a tiny dog ends up with half the bed and most of the covers, but she's cute, so she gets away with it."

Erik laughed. "I've been trying to teach her to sleep in her little dog bed, but she cries and I'm a sucker."

"I would say you've spoiled her, but I have a feeling she was the princess of the house before she managed to get herself lost."

He didn't like to think about Peanut being lost, in no small part because it made him think about somebody out there looking for her. Remembering she wasn't really his dog wasn't something he cared to dwell on.

The show caught their attention for a few minutes and they laughed together at the on-screen antics. Then his phone buzzed in his pocket and he knew before he pulled it out that he'd see his father's name on the screen. And he could tell Andie knew it, too, because she tensed a little and then started to pull away. This was the part where she'd be left to watch TV or read a book while he spent at least an hour on the phone, dissecting his game with his dad.

He used the arm around her shoulders to pull her back into his embrace while he used his other hand to decline the call. Then he powered the phone down and tossed it on the side table. He knew what mistakes he'd made. He knew the Marauders' weaknesses. And there was plenty of time to rehash every move he'd made on the ice.

Tonight, he had the woman he loved next to him and if he was going to keep her there, he had to make these moments count. He needed to prove to her that there was room in his life for hockey *and* her.

As Andie snuggled against his side again, a small smile

curving her mouth, Peanut snuffled and licked his hand once before going to back to sleep.

And the dog, too, he thought. There was room for more than the game in his life.

5

The next morning at the office, Andie hung up the phone and dropped her face into her hands. A family was getting the best Christmas gift ever—their beloved family pet had been found, cared for by a soft-hearted hockey player and would be coming home happy and healthy just in time for the holiday.

She had to tell Erik. As much as she didn't think he fully understood yet the time and care a dog required, he'd gotten attached to Peanut and it wasn't going to be easy for him to let her go. Her duty was to her patient, though, and not the human she'd attached herself to. And it was in Peanut's best interest to be returned to the family who loved and was desperately missing her.

Time wasn't going to make it any easier, so she punched in his number—though she remembered it, she refused to put him back in her contacts—and waited for his voice mail message to kick in.

"Hello?" His voice surprised her to the point of being speechless. "Andie? Are you there?"

"Yeah. I'm here." She cleared her throat. "I wasn't expecting you to pick up, so it took me off guard."

"I'm waiting to see the physical therapist, which means I'm not actually doing anything except wasting time I could be on the ice."

The way he raised his voice toward the end signaled his words were for the benefit of somebody within earshot, rather than her. "So you've got a minute?"

"Yeah. I have all the minutes you need since they can sit and wait for me as long as I've been sitting here waiting for them."

His impatience for anything—or anybody—that kept him off the ice was clear in his voice and she hated to add to his bad mood, but she didn't have a choice. "I was calling to tell you we found Peanut's family."

The silence went on so long, Andie found herself wishing she'd told him in person so she could hold his hand or give him a hug or something.

"Okay," he said finally. "Were they looking for her?"

"Yes. The parents don't really do a lot online and the kids are young enough so they're not really into the social media thing, so they were looking the old-fashioned way. Posters. Calling shelters. Stuff like that. But they really were looking for her. They were visiting family and somebody left the door open and it was a while before the kids realized she was missing."

"Kids." He said the word in a flat voice and she knew what that meant. He might have been tempted to fight for Peanut, but taking a dog away from children wasn't something he could bring himself to do. "Did you let them know I found her?"

"Not yet. I wanted to tell you first." She paused, kicking herself again for doing this over the phone. "If it's easier for you, you can bring her to the clinic and then her family can come pick her up there."

"She whimpers when she thinks I'm going to leave her alone. It'll be easier to leave her if she's getting loved on by her kids. Know what I mean?" He cleared his throat harshly, and her heart broke a little more for him. "Will you go with me? To drop her off, I mean."

"Of course," she said without thinking. He needed somebody and she didn't think he'd ask anybody else.

"I should be out of here in a couple hours, so find out what time works for them and let me know."

"Okay. I'm sorry, Erik."

"She'll be happier with her family," he said roughly. "And I can focus on my game instead of worrying about her."

After they hung up, Andie leaned back in her chair with a sigh. Of course he would hide his emotions behind the veil of the game. That's what he did. He kept his emotions at bay by hiding behind hockey. And when emotions did get in and get messy, he did more hiding behind the hockey. It always circled back to the ice with Erik.

And she would do well to remember that.

It worked out his house was between the clinic and Peanut's real house, so she drove that far instead of him driving in circles. Traffic was a bitch, though, so he was in the car and ready to go when she arrived, and she had to pick Peanut up from her spot in the shotgun seat in order to get in. Once the little dog was curled on her lap, Andie looked at the stuff in the back seat. Everything he'd bought for the dog was piled there, and there was a lot of it.

She'd already sent him the address by text message and he had it punched into his navigation system. It was almost an hour to where Peanut belonged, and they spent most of it in silence masked by the radio. Every time Erik reached over to stroke the dog, Andie's heart broke a little bit more.

Luckily, the family was too busy fussing over Peanut— whose real name was Cookie—to recognize Erik, who hid his grief by making multiple trips from the car with the dog's belongings. He refused to accept any money from Peanut's owner, and then it was time to say goodbye. When Peanut licked Erik's hand, Andie's eyes burned and she was afraid the dog would try to jump into his arms, but after that last gesture of thanks, the little dog ran back to the little girls she clearly loved.

The ride back to Erik's house was even more oppressive, and she noticed he had the radio on a rock station instead of something playing holiday music. Since he loved Christmas songs, it was a pretty good indicator of how bad his mood was.

She went inside with him, even though he wasn't the best company at the moment. In her experience, it was the times people were bad company that they needed company the most. Especially people like Erik, who weren't really good at expressing emotions.

He paused in the kitchen and looked around before sighing, and she knew the house probably felt empty and quiet to him. Peanut hadn't been very big size-wise, but she'd brought a lot of heart into the home.

"You saved her," Andie said quietly, standing next to him at the kitchen island. "And now she's back with a family who loves her very much, thanks to you."

"My business manager's going to look into funding medical expenses for dogs who don't have any people, like you were talking about. And when I retire and don't have to go out on the road anymore, I'm going to go to the shelter and find another dog who'll love me like Peanut did." Then he shrugged one shoulder. "Although, you were probably right. Peanut loves everybody."

"No." She put her hand on his arm. "Peanut likes everybody, but she *loved* you. You were her champion."

"And everybody loves a champion."

She started to smile, but the bitter undertone made her look at him. "What's that supposed to mean?"

"What?" He shook his head as if he hadn't even heard himself speak. "Nothing."

Everybody loves a champion. Andie had spent just enough time with Lamont Burke to guess those weren't Erik's words. They were his father's. He'd always been his son's number one fan and Erik always credited his father for his success, but she wondered if either of them recognized the damage it had done.

Erik's value was tied to his success at hockey. In his mind, at least. And seemingly his father's mind, as well.

"So you're off for the holidays now, right?" she asked, hoping to change the subject to something a little more cheerful.

"Yeah, we have a few days with no games, but I wouldn't say I'm off, exactly."

"When are you ever?" She tried to keep the sorrow and regret at the truth of his life out of her voice, but she didn't think she succeeded very well.

"On top of the regular games, we've got the Winter Classic right around the corner, and then the All-Star Game." He shook his head. "I'll be spending most of the holidays watching film with my dad."

Everything in Erik's kitchen was digital, and yet Andie imagined seconds ticking on an old-fashioned clock as the silence stretched on. She didn't want to say anything rash when he was already emotionally vulnerable. Hell, she wasn't sure what she could say, anyway. It's not as if she hadn't known going in that hockey was, and always would be, his first love.

"I should go," she finally said in a soft voice. "I have a lot on my plate and you obviously have games to prepare for."

"Seeing the family for Christmas?" At least he sounded mildly interested.

"Not this year. Chelsea wants to fly home, so I'll be spending more time than usual at the clinic." She forced herself to smile. "I need to rest and wrap presents when I get the chance."

Erik scrubbed a hand over his face. "I'm probably not great company right now, anyway. And I'm supposed to go to Kristen's tomorrow to have dinner with her and Cross or something after I stop at my dad's, so I should get some rest."

He kissed her goodbye, holding her close and promising to talk to her soon, but as she backed her car out of his driveway, Andie couldn't help wondering if it would be for the last time. She'd missed him for the last year, sometimes so much she cried herself to sleep, but she still wasn't ready to come second to his job, no matter what his job was.

LAMONT BURKE LIVED in a very nice condo by the beach on the South Shore, close enough to stop by Erik's when he felt the need, but just far enough away so he always called first. It had cost enough to have Erik's financial manager popping antacids, but Erik had told him he couldn't put a price on what his father had done for him over the course of his career.

For the first time, though, walking into his dad's house

on Christmas Eve made Erik vaguely uncomfortable. It wasn't a home. It was a shrine to the career of Erik Burke of the Boston Marauders.

Maybe it was having been in Kristen's house earlier in the week. There were pictures of Cross on the ice, of course. Hoisting the Cup. But there were also pictures of their families. And pictures of Cross and Kristen together. What had struck Erik that day was that the picture of his sister and her boyfriend walking on the beach, laughing together, had been in the biggest frame and was the focal point. Not Cross's career, but the life they were building together.

There was only one picture of Erik in his father's living room that didn't show him in his uniform. He was wearing a suit and had been at the awards night. There wasn't even a prom picture because he hadn't gone to prom. He'd either been on the ice or training or talking about training.

"I want a picture of Andie and I walking on the beach hanging over the back of my couch."

"What are you talking about?" His dad had been opening a beer, and he handed it to Erik, who shook his head. "Who's Andie?"

"Andrea." When Lamont just continued with the blank look, Erik felt something inside of him crack open. "Andrea, Dad. We were together for months. Dark, curly hair? Ring any bells? The woman I love and would have asked to marry me, except she wasn't willing to take a back seat to a sport so we broke up a year ago."

"Good for you. You have a gift. You were put on this earth to play hockey and you can't throw that away."

His father had said those words to him a million times. Erik wouldn't have been surprised if Lamont learned to embroider just so he could cross-stitch it on a pillow for his son's bed. It was the sentiment that had driven Erik for his entire life—from the time he learned to skate through high school and into the big leagues—and pushed him to be faster, stronger and smarter. He did have a gift. He was a freaking great hockey player.

"No," he said, surprising them both. Erik could hardly believe the word had come out of his own mouth, but as soon as he said it, he knew it was right. "I have a natural *skill* for hockey that I've honed with years of training and hard work, but I was put on this earth to *live my life*. To live and to love, Dad. Hockey is my passion and hockey is my job, but it is *not* my life. And I walked away from the *real* gift I was given."

If he'd thought about the words, he might not have had the guts to say them out loud. His father had worked his ass off since the day Erik's first hockey coach said he was born to play hockey. That he had a gift and could go pro. His dad had moved, taking a job that payed less in an area that cost more to position Erik on a better hockey team. His dad had sacrificed. His sister had sacrificed. And Erik had strived his entire career to honor those sacrifices.

But at what cost?

He was ready to admit the price he'd paid to live up to the expectations of his father, his coaches and himself. Picturing the look on Andie's face when he'd said he was busy over the holidays because he had to focus on the games ahead made it hard to breathe and he finally understood. There hadn't been any room for her and he'd never made an effort to put her first.

"I have to go, Dad."

"You just got here. And the Winter Classic is—"

"A hockey game." Erik was already pulling on his coat. "I don't think—I *hope*—I won't be back tonight, but I'll see you tomorrow."

Erik left before Lamont could get over his surprise and use all the familiar phrases to get back into his head. He called Andie's number from the car, but got no answer. And when he drove by her apartment building, her car wasn't in its space. Then he remembered she was working extra at the clinic to cover for Chelsea.

Not the best place for what he had to say, but he wasn't going to wait any more. The young receptionist was back at the desk, watching a Christmas comedy on a tablet when he walked in.

"Sorry," she said, tapping the pause button. "We don't have regular appointments this week because we always get bombed with dogs that ate something they shouldn't and cats that get hold of ribbon, but it's slow today."

"Is Andie around?"

"She was checking on a cat we have staying over for observation, but I think she's in her office now." Before Erik could tell her he knew the way, she'd hit a button. "Andie? Peanut's dad is here to see you."

That hurt. *Peanut's dad.* Obviously the news about her going home hadn't spread. But rather than focusing on his loss, he thought about the joyful reunion of Peanut and her girls until Andie appeared from out back.

"Erik." She looked confused. "I thought you were going to your dad's. You didn't find another dog, did you?"

"Not yet, but I think visiting some shelters will be in my near future." He shoved his hands in his pockets, jittery suddenly and not sure what else to do with them. "Can we talk somewhere for a minute?"

"Sure." She nodded her head and he followed her back to her office. It was even smaller than the exam rooms, but he peeled off his coat and shut the door.

Andie looked at his face, her brows furrowing. "What's wrong?"

"I'm sorry."

"For?"

This was so damn hard, but hopefully worth it. "I'm sorry I made you feel like you weren't as important as hockey to me. No, wait. You didn't just feel like that. It was me. I didn't make you more important than hockey. And I'm sorry."

Tears shimmered in her eyes. "I don't really know what to say."

"I love you." His throat tightened and he cleared his throat. "I loved you then, and I let you walk away. I still love you—I will always love you because you are my one—and I hurt you again, when I used hockey to avoid dealing with giving Peanut back. I should have let you in."

"I still love you, too, Erik. I never stopped."

His pulse quickened and he had to take a deep breath. "I want us to be together again, Andie. Forever. I'll retire right now. I'll call everybody I've got to call and tell them I'm not playing anymore because I found a woman who's more important to me than anything, including hockey."

"Erik, I..."

He pulled out his phone. "I mean it. I'll call right here and now."

"I don't want you to retire. That's never what I wanted." She slid her arms around his waist, tilting her head back to look up at him. "I never asked you to give up hockey. I would *never* have asked you to do that. All I wanted was for you to be present and really *with* me when you were with me. I had a place in your bed and I think I had a place in your heart, but I never fully occupied your mind."

"I get it. You tried telling me before and I didn't really listen."

"What's changed between then and now?"

"What's changed? Everything. What's changed is that I've spent the last year without you in my life. And because I had you in my life, I know what I'm missing. I know what it felt like with you and I know what it feels like without you, and being without you sucks." He sighed and wrapped his arms around her. "That's all I've got Andie. I love you and being without you really sucks."

"Being without you really sucks, too."

He kissed her, holding her as tightly as he could without crushing her. Her kisses always rocked his world, but this one was different—better—because she was his again. He'd gotten a second shot and he wasn't going to blow it this time.

"I don't have a ring yet," he said when they finally came up for air, "but I want you to be mine forever, Andie. I want you to share my life and my home and...everything. A dog."

"Definitely a dog." She stretched up on her toes to kiss him again. "Yes, Erik. And Merry Christmas."

ALSO BY SHANNON STACEY

To see the complete list of titles by Shannon Stacey, visit the Books tab on her website, shannonstacey.com.

Hockey Romances

Here We Go – Book 1

A Second Shot – Book 1.5

The Boston Fire Series

A contemporary romance series about tough, dedicated (and sexy) firefighters!

Heat Exchange – Book 1

Controlled Burn – Book 2

Fully Ignited – Book 3

Hot Response – Book 4

Under Control – Book 5

Flare Up – Book 6

The Boys of Fall Series

A contemporary romance series about going home again.

Under The Lights – Book 1

Defending Hearts – Book 2

Homecoming – Book 3

The Kowalski Series

A contemporary romance series full of family, fun and falling in love.

Exclusively Yours – Book 1

Undeniably Yours – Book 2

Yours To Keep – Book 3

All He Ever Needed – Book 4

All He Ever Desired – Book 5

All He Ever Dreamed – Book 6

Alone With You – Novella 6.5

Love A Little Sideways – Book 7

Taken With You – Book 8

Falling For Max – Book 9

What It Takes – Book 10

Cedar Street Novellas

Fun, tropey hijinks in a small town!

One Summer Weekend – Book 1

One Christmas Eve – Book 2

The Devlin Group Series

This action-adventure romance series follows the men and women of the Devlin Group, a privately owned rogue agency unhindered by red tape and jurisdiction.

72 Hours – Book 1

On The Edge – Book 2

No Surrender – Book 3

No Place To Hide – Book 4

Christmas Novellas

Holiday Sparks

Mistletoe & Margaritas

Snowbound With the CEO

Her Holiday Man

In the Spirit

Holiday With A Twist

Hold Her Again

Historical Westerns

Taming Eliza Jane – Book 1

Becoming Miss Becky – Book 2

Also Available

A Fighting Chance

Heart of the Storm

Slow Summer Kisses

Kiss Me Deadly

ABOUT THE AUTHOR

The *New York Times* and *USA Today* bestselling author of over forty romances, Shannon Stacey lives with her husband and two sons in New England. Her favorite activities are writing romance and really random tweets with her dogs curled up at her side. She loves books, coffee, Boston sports and watching way too much TV.

facebook.com/shannonstacey.authorpage
twitter.com/shannonstacey
instagram.com/shannonstacey

Made in the USA
Las Vegas, NV
12 June 2022

50131745R10125